A REAL COWBOY FOR CHRISTMAS

CHRISTMAS

A WYOMING REBELS NOVEL

STEPHANIE ROWE

SBD PRESS

COPYRIGHT

A REAL COWBOY FOR CHRISTMAS (a *Wyoming Rebels* novel).
Copyright © 2017 by Stephanie Rowe.

BOOKS BY STEPHANIE ROWE

CONTEMPORARY ROMANCE

**For a complete list of Stephanie's books, go to
www.stephanierowe.com**

ACKNOWLEDGMENTS

Special thanks to my beta readers and the Rockstars. You guys are the best! There are so many to thank by name, more than I could count, but here are those who I want to called out specially for all they did to help this book come to life: Malinda Davis Diehl, Leslie Barnes, Kayla Bartley, Alencia Bates Salters, Alyssa Bird, Donna Bossert, Jean Bowden, Shell Bryce, Ashley Cuesta, Denise Fluhr, Valerie Glass, Heidi Hoffman, Jeanne Stone, Guinevere Jones, Dottie Jones, Janet Juengling-Snell, Deb Julienne, Bridget Koan, Helen Loyal, Felicia Low Mikoll, Phyllis Marshall, Suzanne Mayer, Jodi Moore, Ashlee Murphy, Elizabeth Neal, Judi Pflughoeft, Carol Pretorius, Kasey Richardson, Caryn Santee, Amber Ellison Shriver, Summer Steelman, Regina Thomas, and Linda Watson. Special thanks to my family, who I love with every fiber of my heart and soul. And to AER, who is my world. Love you so much, baby girl! And to Joe, who teaches me every day what romance and true really is. I love you, babe!

For Guinevere, for telling me this book needed to be written, and for being right. I am so much more because I have you in my corner, cheering me on, pushing me to stretch, encouraging me to believe in myself. You are AMAZING and I am so grateful to have you in my life! I love ya, babe!

CHAPTER 1

A deathbed promise should never involve snow, subzero temperatures, and family who don't know you even exist, and sure as hell don't know you're coming.

Especially a deathbed promise given in front of one's six-year-old daughter, who won't ever let you forget your oath. Like, ever. Not even for one headache-laden, frostbitten-toes moment.

"Mom!" The six-year-old in question tugged on Jaimi Hamilton's hand, apparently not remotely concerned about the wind that was knifing through their clothes. Because that was how six-year-olds operated. They never felt cold, unless it was eighty degrees and they wanted to leave the park the *minute* the attractive, single dad with decent moral standards and a car that actually worked showed up. "Do you see them? Are they here?"

Jaimi squatted down so she was level with her daughter, her heart tugging at the way Emily's blue eyes sparkled in the wintry snow. She gently pulled Emily's stocking cap lower over her forehead. "Baby cakes, remember. This is a secret

1

mission. They can't ever know we're here for them, unless we decide to reveal our true identity, right?"

Emily's lower lip jutted out. "What if I don't want to be a spy?"

"We have to be spies. What if they're evil, and we have to stop their plan to steal toys from all the children in the world on Christmas morning? Then we don't want them to know who we are, right?"

Emily giggled and rolled her eyes. "They don't have a plan to steal toys from all the children in the world."

"Really? You're so sure about that?" Jaimi gave her daughter her most skeptical look. "How do we know until we spy on them for a while?"

Emily put her hands on her hips and eyed her mom. "Grandma would never tell us to come to Wyoming to find them, unless they were nice. Don't you trust Gram?"

Jaimi laughed. "Sweetie, no one *ever* trusts Gram if they know what's good for them." Wait. Not *trusts*. Trust*ed*. Because Gram was gone now. God, she felt like she'd never get used to that fact.

Laughter bubbled out of Emily. "Gram was such trouble."

"That she was." A lump formed in Jaimi's throat, but she quickly swallowed it away. She'd promised her mom that there would be no tears. Life was too short for tears and regret. Every moment was a gift to be treasured. "And so are you."

Emily's grin widened. "Gram says you're trouble, too."

"That's been my lifelong goal, so I'm still working on it." Jaimi pulled off her glove and held up her hand. "Trouble-making girls rock the world, right?"

"Right!" Emily whipped off her pink fuzzy mitten and hooked her pinkie around Jaimi's. "I swear to cause trouble my whole life," she said with a solemn giggle as they squeezed pinkies. "Just like you and Gram."

"And I swear to continue to cause trouble my whole life, just like *you* and Gram." God, how many times had she made that oath with her mom over the years? A thousand times? And then, after Emily had been born, it had been the three of them...until two months ago. Now it was back down to two.

Two pinkies were not nearly as good as three when it came to pinkie swears.

Emily beamed at her. "They'll love us, Mom. We're amazing like that."

Jaimi couldn't help but smile at her daughter's self-confidence. Her number one goal as a mom had always been to raise a daughter who lived life on her own terms, who would never be held back by what anyone thought of her. It meant she had a little hellion on her hands at times, but she'd never trade a second of chaos for a daughter who shrank from who she was, who she wanted to be, or what anyone thought of her.

In terms of embracing her badass self, the pupil had far surpassed the teacher long ago, and was turning out to be a lot like her Gram, which was awesome. Jaimi, on the other hand, wasn't nearly the self-confident, fuck-the-world, mover and shaker that her daughter thought she was. But hey, that was her little secret, right? As far as Emily was concerned, Jaimi was everything she told Emily to be. So, she smiled. "Of course they'll love us. Who wouldn't want two fabulous girls appearing on their doorstep the week before Christmas and announcing they're family that no one ever knew existed, right?" Oh, God. Just the idea of that made her stomach knot. What on earth had her mom been thinking, making Jaimi promise to make this trip? She hadn't specifically made Jaimi promise to actually *introduce* herself, however, so Jaimi was holding tight to that little loophole.

"Totally!" Emily clapped her hands. "Can we do it today? You have the address, right? To their *huuuge* ranch? What if we moved onto the ranch? Can I get a horse? I could become a barrel racer—"

"Slow down, cheetah-girl. We're not moving here. We're just here for Christmas vacation, and we both have to be back at school after New Year's."

Emily wrinkled her nose. "You don't like teaching. I heard you telling Gram. Why do you teach if you don't like it? You always tell me to follow my heart, and you're not." Emily set her hands on her hips and glared at Jaimi, apparently completely offended by her mom's failure to deliver.

Sigh. Maybe she should have focused more on raising a wimpy child who hid in her room all day after all... She tweaked her daughter's nose. "I do like teaching, and I keep teaching because it works perfectly because we're in school at the same time, so you don't need to go to late care, right?"

Emily shrugged. "Late care is fun. Three kids got bloody noses last fall. I missed every one of them. All the blood was cleaned up by the time we had recess the next morning. What fun is that?"

"Recess without blood is definitely a downer." Heaven help her. "But you'll get another chance when we go back there after New Year's. For now, we're here for Christmas, checking out the town, and learning how to enjoy our first Christmas without Gram."

The tenacious little pugilist was not swayed from her agenda. "And we're going to meet our family, right? We're going to go up to them, and you're going to say 'Hey, Chase Stockton, I'm your sister—'"

A few heads turned toward them at Emily's raised voice, and Jaimi quickly interrupted. "Shh, sweetie, I—" She suddenly noticed the sheriff lounging nearby, watching them.

His gaze was intense and hooded, and his casual stance

4

failed to hide the raw strength of his body. His cowboy hat was tipped back, showcasing a strong, whiskered jaw, and dark sunglasses that hid his eyes. But it was clear he was staring right at them, and her stomach jumped again... though she wasn't sure whether it was from fear of being caught before she was ready to declare herself, or because he was just so freaking male. His jeans were faded, and his long jacket was open, flapping about his calves, as if he didn't feel the cold at all. There was something untamed and unruly about him, as if he were the kind of man who lived life without walls, exactly how she wanted so badly to be.

He nodded at her, and she suddenly realized she was staring at him. Heat flared in her cheeks, and she dragged her gaze off him and back to Emily. "We need to be top secret, Em." The Stocktons were well-known in Rogue Valley, and she didn't need the sheriff, or anyone else, alerting them that two out-of-towners were talking about being their long-lost family before Jaimi had a chance to figure out how she wanted to handle it. "We might or might not introduce ourselves, remember? We're spies right now, until we decide whether we want them to know who we are. If they aren't worthy, they don't get to know us, right?"

Emily met her gaze. "They'll be worthy." There was absolute conviction in her voice, which alarmed Jaimi.

She realized the little minx was planning to take control of the situation. *No way.* Some things in life were far more complicated than a six-year-old could grasp, and this was one of them. Curses to Gram for bringing Emily into this! Jaimi grasped her daughter's hands and squeezed gently. "Sweetie, I need you to make me a promise. Some people in this world aren't so nice. We don't know if the Stocktons are nice, and we don't know whether they would fit us. So, promise me you won't mention their names again unless we're alone, and you won't introduce us, until we both decide together that it's the right decision. We're a team, remember?"

Emily sighed, but nodded. "I promise, but Mom, it'll be okay. Gram said you'd be scared, and I had to keep telling you it would be okay so your inner wimp wouldn't win out. So, it will be okay, 'kay?"

Jaimi's brows shot up. "My inner wimp?"

"Yes, Gram says we all have one, but yours is really loud and obnoxious and it sometimes needs to be smacked around to make it shut up."

Jaimi burst out laughing at her mom's words coming out of a six-year-old's mouth. "God, I love you, kiddo."

Emily beamed at her. "I love you, too, Mom." She reached her hand into her parka pocket and pulled out a photograph. She held it up, and scanned the crowds passing by them. "I brought Chase's photo. Do you see him? Let's start spying—"

"You brought one of the photos Gram had?" Jaimi snatched it out of her daughter's hand. Good God. They were going to look like stalkers! "I'll take that." She looked around, needing to distract her daughter. They were on the edge of the grounds of the Rogue Valley Christmas Festival, and there were people everywhere, tromping through the snow, wearing Santa hats, and overflowing with happy laughter on this opening afternoon of the three-day celebration. "Oh...look! Reindeer!"

"Where?" Emily spun around, her eyes widening when she saw the pen of reindeer across the way. Christmas lights twinkled on the fence, and two of Santa's elves were giving out food pellets for the children to feed the animals. "Do you think Rudolph is there? Can we see?" She took off in a sprint, not even waiting for Jaimi.

Jaimi sighed, and sat back on her heels, watching her

daughter dart across the dirt road, effortlessly dodging crowds until she reached the fence around the reindeer pen. Emily grabbed the middle bar and climbed right up, moving with alarming speed and determination. Dear God, was she going to climb *into* the pen? "Em! Get down!" Jaimi jumped up and started running toward her. "Emily!"

Suddenly, she heard a horn blast, and she glanced to her right. A huge tractor was bearing down on her, only feet away. "Oh, shit—"

Something suddenly hit her hard from the side, thrusting her out of the path of the tractor. She landed hard on the frozen ground, gasping as two strong arms dragged her across the gravelly earth, jerking her trailing feet out of the way of the massive tires just as they crunched by.

She gasped, frozen, as she watched the enormous tractor roll by, towing a trailer filled with hay bales and curious people, who were leaning over the side, gawking at her. Dear God. She'd almost been *crushed*. That would have made for an extremely sucky first-Christmas-without-Gram, positive attitude notwithstanding.

Her lungs heaved, trying to catch her breath, as she became gradually aware that she was lying on top of a warm body, not the hard ground, and that those arms were still locked around her waist.

She looked down at the hands clasped around her belly, and saw the worn black cuffs of a certain calf-length jacket she had just been gawking at a few minutes ago. Oh, *crap*. The hot sheriff had saved her? Heat rose in her cheeks as she twisted around to look behind her.

Sure enough, playing the role of her landing pad, was the same untamed, intensely male sheriff who had been watching her so carefully just a moment ago. It was his hard, hot body beneath her, and his booted foot between her calves. He grinned, flashing her a smile that made heat tingle all the way to her frozen toes. "Welcome to Rogue Valley. My name's Sheriff Wilson..." He paused. "But you can call me Dane."

CHAPTER 2

*D*ane Wilson wasn't going to lie: the next time Roger Ubanks, the driver of that tractor, got stopped for a traffic violation, he was going to give the guy a free pass. Maybe not just the next time. Roger might have just earned a lifetime of driving like a maniac with no repercussions, because Dane owed him.

Big time.

Because the woman he'd been watching for the last ten minutes was now sitting on his lap, staring at him, and he hadn't had to do anything but be a hero to make it happen, thanks to Roger's hayride fail.

The look of shock on her face was adorable, and so was the red tint to her cold cheeks. The feel of her bum nestled against his thighs? It had been a long time since he'd had a woman parked in that spot, and it felt damn good. No, *it* didn't feel good. *She* felt damn good, which was why he hadn't rolled her off him the moment they'd landed.

He wasn't going to dislodge her until she decided it was time, and so far, she wasn't moving. In fact, instead of getting up, she'd twisted around in his arms to look at him, giving him his first close-up view of her face. Her white faux fur hat hid all but a few tendrils of dark, curly hair, but her dark brown eyes were huge and luminous against her gorgeous brown skin. She had no makeup on, and there were tiny lines around the corners of her eyes...and she took his breath away.

He grinned wider, glad as hell that she'd taken off her glove long enough for him to see that she wasn't wearing a ring on her left hand. Otherwise, it would be damned awkward that he was enjoying her being on his lap so much.

He was too old for awkward, so this was starting off well. "And you are...?" he prompted, unwilling to take the chance that she would disentangle herself before he'd gotten her name.

She blinked. "Jaimi. Jaimi Hamilton."

Kindness.

That was the first word that popped into Dane's head when he heard her voice. Warmth. The kind of human being who was worth keeping around, because she'd make everyone around her feel better, simply by being herself.

He'd seen her smile at her daughter, and that beaming radiance had transfixed him. But now that he'd heard her voice, now that she was looking right at him, now that he could see the sprinkle of freckles across her cheeks, and the tiny scar on the bridge of her nose, and the adorably imperfect crookedness of her two front teeth, he was thinking he was pretty close to being a goner.

He'd been looking for the right woman for a long, damned time, and he'd never found anyone who felt right. He'd met plenty of nice women who thought he had a decent number of redeeming qualities. He'd tried to make things work with a few of them, but nothing had felt the way he'd wanted it to. He'd tried his best to make things happen even when that spark wasn't there, but he'd finally given up. There was no way to make something right that wasn't, so he'd finally let it go. The dream. The hope. He'd just let it the hell go, especially after his sister had called with her news...

Until now.

Until Jaimi Hamilton

He didn't even know her, but something about her had ignited a freaking firestorm inside him. He grinned. "Jaimi Hamilton," he repeated. "That fits you."

She raised her brows. "How on earth would you have any idea if my name fits me? You don't even know me."

Sassy. He loved that. "Because your name makes me think of someone who's fun, upbeat, willing to see the good in life, who loves her kid, and..." His gaze slid to the scar on her nose. "And stays strong even when the shit rains down."

Her eyebrows shot up in surprise, and she tilted her head, studying him more carefully. "Damn, you're good. Have you been stalking me?"

"Only for the last ten minutes, but I'm a sheriff, so I'm really good at judging people instantly and with pinpoint accuracy. It helps me know who to shoot and stuff like that."

She laughed, a riveting burst of giggles so contagious that he couldn't help but chuckle with her. "I am so not someone you should be shooting."

"That's what I concluded as well..." He paused as she turned her head to look past him, no doubt to check on her daughter.

The moment she turned her head, the afternoon light cast shadows across her face, changing the angle of how he saw her. Suddenly, recognition flashed through him, and he realized she looked familiar. "Have we met before?"

She laughed again as she looked back at him. "That's one pickup line that's not going to work with me, unless you've been to Boston. I've spent my whole life there. This is my first trip to this part of the country, and I've been in

Wyoming for about three hours. So, you'll have to try something different. You could compliment me on my daughter. Supposedly, that's a good way to pick up single moms. We have no identity beyond our kids." The dryness of her tone made him laugh again.

"Yeah," he said, "the bond between you and your daughter is obvious, but I'm not buying the idea that it would be easy to trick you into surrendering to my charms. I'm super charming though. It would be a good choice for you to fall for me."

She grinned. "Charm is wasted on me. I like bitter, autocratic men with no sense of humor, so you might as well give up now if you consider yourself charming or adorable, or anything like that." Her gaze flicked again toward her daughter, and again, he had a flash of recognition. "As a single mom, I have no time for men, so you need to just bail on the pick-up lines. It's never going to happen."

He frowned. Something about the angle of her face when she turned away from him looked so damned familiar. He *knew* that he'd met her before, but when? And if he had, how the hell would he have forgotten her? She was like a firestorm of sunlight, and he couldn't imagine he would have failed to notice her before. "I'm not going to lie," he said. "I definitely plan to hit on you until you agree that I'm fantastic and worth going on a date with, but I haven't started my nefarious assault yet. I actually do think you look familiar. I'm sure I've seen you before."

Her gaze settled on his, and for a long moment, silence reigned between them. A little furrow appeared between her brows, and he was gratified to see that she believed he was serious, and not just playing her. "I really have never been here before," she said. "Have you been to New England?"

He shook his head. "I grew up here and never left. You aren't friends with my sister, Zoey Wilson, are you? She lives in Boston." *Zoey*. Just mentioning her made a darkness settle over him. He had no idea how to help her.

Jaimi's gaze settled on his. "What's wrong?"

Shit. He didn't want to go there. He didn't want to bring that into this moment of sunshine. He quickly shoved his worry about his sister aside and focused on Jaimi. "Nothing. It's all good." He cocked his head, studying her face. The longer he looked at her, the more familiar she seemed. He *knew* he knew her. "So, if you've never been here, what about your mom or dad? Or a sister? Maybe you look like your family—"

A look of alarm flashed across her face, and she suddenly disentangled herself from him so fast, he had to jerk his knee to the side to protect his nuts from being smashed by her elbow. She was on her feet in a split second. "I need to go get my daughter. She's over there—" She waved her arm in a sweeping motion that pretty much encompassed the entire western half of the festival grounds, then she turned and literally bolted away from him.

Huh.

Dane propped himself up on his elbows, not bothering to get up as he watched her frantic flight through the crowds toward her daughter, who was safely engaged in some sort of animated discussion with one of Santa's elves. He laughed softly, still cracking up that he'd gotten Zane and Steen Stockton to dress up as elves for part of the festival. It was amazing what having kids had done for those two solitary, hardass bastards.

With their elf costumes on, no one would recognize them as Stocktons, but he knew, and he definitely got some sort of perverse pleasure from knowing they'd had to put on green stockings and red elf pants this morning. He'd caused enough trouble with them over the years that he was one of the few people in town who understood that dressing up as elves to make kids happy was more in line with who they were, rather than being the trouble-making miscreants that had been arrested, along with him, countless times in their youth.

Without the Stocktons, he never would have made it through his own hellish youth, and he knew they felt the same about him. They might not be related by blood, but they were his brothers, and he'd protect them with his life. And, as brothers, it was his duty to make them wear tights, elf hats, and jingle bell bracelets at least once in their lives.

Jaimi reached her daughter, and shot a nervous glance over her shoulder at Dane. When she saw he was still watching her, alarm flickered across her face, and she jerked her gaze away.

Hmm...

He narrowed his eyes, watching her body language as she forced a laugh at something Zane said. She was nervous as hell, and it had happened when he'd recognized her. Her initial denial had been legit, but then something had happened to spook her big time.

He didn't like that she was scared. Hell, he didn't like it when anyone was scared. He was the sheriff to protect people, so it was in his nature. But with Jaimi, it felt personal, not just his job. There was something going on with her, and he didn't like that.

He gestured at Steen to keep her from leaving, and his buddy nodded, shifting his body ever so slightly to pen her and Emily in. Satisfied she wasn't going to get a chance to bolt before he could saunter casually over there, Dane put his hands down to shove himself to his feet. He felt something under his palm and looked down. The square corner of a white paper peeked out from under his thumb, and he realized it was the paper that her daughter had been holding before Jaimi had taken it.

Perfect. He'd use it as an excuse to follow her so he could

give it back, without looking like he was stalking her, because he kinda felt like he was. He was just so damned entranced by her and her nervousness had amped up his reaction to her—

His gaze fell upon the paper as he picked it up, and he frowned. It was a recent photograph of Chase Stockton, taken in the doorway of the Wild Flower Café, which was owned by Travis Stockton's wife, Lissa. Why would she have a photograph of Chase?

Narrowing his eyes, he flipped it over. On the back was the address of the Stockton ranch, and the names of all nine Stockton brothers. Chase. Steen. Zane. Maddox. Ryder. Travis. Logan. Quintin. Hell, she even had Caleb's name on there, and no one had been able to track him down in years.

He looked back up at Jaimi, chatting with two of the men whose names she had on that photograph. Did she know she was talking to them? Protectiveness surged through Dane again, and this time, it wasn't for an out-of-towner with a lack of basic tractor safety skills. It was for the men he called family.

Who the hell was Jaimi Hamilton, and why the hell was she in town, with a list of the Stocktons, their address, and Chase's photo?

He didn't know, but he sure as hell was going to find out.

And he was going to find out now.

CHAPTER 3

*O*kay, so that had been insanely awkward.

Jaimi tried not to look over her shoulder at the sheriff she'd just literally fled from. He was a sheriff, for heaven's sake. How was he *not* going to think that behavior was weird? She might as well have grabbed a Sharpie and written "I have big secrets I'm hiding" on her forehead.

It was his fault. He'd been so damn charming that she'd forgotten to put up walls and keep him dancing out of range. She'd wanted to connect with him, to let his smile make her feel good, to let him flirt with her a little.

He was handsome. He had a great smile. He'd saved her from pancake-ville. And he had the faintest hint of shadows in his eyes, which made him human. Yes, she was a committed single mom who was obsessively devoted to giving up everything that mattered to her to ensure the well-being of her kid, in accordance with every holier-than-thou-mom social media post that crossed her feed. However, she was also a sex-starved, relationship-challenged woman who wasn't immune to a man like Dane Wilson sending his charms her way.

Which had made her panic and act like a complete idiot.

"Mommy!" Emily tugged on her hand. "Did you hear what Santa's elf just said? Did you?"

Jaimi focused on her daughter, and the massively-broad-shouldered elf who was crouching in front of her. "Sorry, I was admiring the reindeer's tail." *What?* Admiring a reindeer's *tail?* What kind of lunatic lie was that? She might as well have said, "Hey, I have a fetish for furry butts." Good God. That sheriff had completely rattled her. She cleared her throat, and forced her attention on her daughter, trying not to notice whether the elves had marked her as crazy yet. "What did he say?"

Emily beamed at her, excitement dancing in her eyes. "He said there's a concert starting in an hour. Travis Turner! I love him! Can we go? Please, please, please? Can we go?"

Oh, man. Right now, she was feeling like heading back to the hotel and regrouping, not dealing with a bunch of swooning women ogling the massive country music star... How had they gotten such a huge headliner to perform at a local Christmas festival, anyway? Maybe Rogue Valley was more than the tiny town she'd driven through on the way to the festival. Or maybe Travis Turner had run over someone with his truck when driving through town and he'd been blackmailed into performing. Yeah, probably more likely...

Not that she had time to wonder about the booking talents of the local organizers, right? She had to stay focused on important tasks, like avoiding a certain sheriff who was probably Googling her right now. "I think we'll skip it, sweetie. Concerts can get pretty rowdy—"

"Not this one." The elf grinned up at Jaimi, flashing her a smile that was almost, but not quite, as charming as Dane's. "It's a family show. It'll be okay for her."

She had a sudden urge to jam the toe of her boot into that

disarming grin. "I appreciate the recommendation, but I think we'll head back to our hotel—"

"Moooom!" Emily tugged on her hand. "I know he's your favorite! Please!"

Travis Turner *had* been her favorite, until attending his show meant staying within pouncing range of a certain hot sheriff with too much intelligence for her convenience. Hadn't Dane heard about guys who had rocks for brains behind their pretty faces and delicious muscles? Apparently not. The man needed to get out more, apparently. "We need to get dinner," she said firmly, gripping Em's hand and turning to leave...which put her facing Dane, who was striding directly toward her, a dark expression on his face.

His gaze drilled into her, freezing her in her frostbitten, snowbound tracks. Crap. He looked mad. Why? What had she done, other than almost neuter him with her elbow? Because yes, she had noticed that close call, and was horrified that she hadn't even managed to apologize before fleeing.

Something white by his hip caught her eye, and she stared at it. It took her a full moment to recognize it, then dread clogged her throat. He had the picture of Chase in his hand. Double crap. No wonder he looked mad. She gripped Emily's hand. "We definitely gotta go—" She managed only one step, before the other elf stepped in front of her, blocking her path.

She stopped. "Seriously? Are you guys tag-teaming me or something?"

He grinned at her, a smile that looked suspiciously similar to the first elf. He had a small cross hanging from his left ear, which just didn't look elf-like at all, right? More like a biker. "If you're looking for dinner," he said, with a casualness so deliberate that she didn't buy it for even a split second, "there's a barbeque during the concert as well. Travis Turner donated the food, and there's enough for the whole town." He smiled at Emily. "Do you like burgers?"

She beamed at him, as of course she would. Small children were experts at being treacherous little traitors when it suited them. "I love burgers. And fries. Are there fries?" She lowered her voice to a whisper that Santa could have heard even from the North Pole. "My mom makes me eat broccoli instead of fries."

"Yes, I do." Jaimi grimaced, watching Dane get closer. The man knew how to navigate crowds far too well, and he was barely slowed by all the people wanting to chat with him. Even when he spoke to them, he kept his gaze pinned on her, which, she had to admit, was both electrifying and alarming. Hot cowboy staring at her: awesome and a little terrifying. Suspicious and pissed off law enforcement officer bearing down on her: not at all awesome and definitely terrifying.

Terrifying either way, which meant sticking around was a poor choice on any level...And he was getting close! Panic closed in, and she realized she had only seconds to make a break for it. Of course, she could just plant her feet and decide that he was hunting her down because he was going to propose a moonlit sleigh ride snuggled under a fuzzy, insanely warm blanket while two gorgeous snow-white horses drew them along.

He held up the photo.

Shit. No sleigh ride intended. She wasn't staying around to be interrogated. She was a horrible liar at her best, and she was too cold for even that level of unenviable performance. Decision made. Time to bail. She squeezed her daughter's hand. "Okay, Em, you win. Let's head back to the hotel and get some warmer clothes, and then we'll come back for the barbeque and the concert. But we'll have to be quick, so let's run." As Emily squealed with delight, Jaimi tried to step around the elf, but the oversized elf, who was way too strong and big to possibly fool any child, moved with her, still blocking her path.

"Excuse me," she said, trying to hide her desperation. "but we really need to go—"

"Jaimi."

Dane's deep voice made her teeth clench, though she wasn't sure if it was from a shot of stark terror, or the flashback to landing on his lap after he saved her. His voice was so deep, and so delicious, and so tempting...

Damn him.

She grimaced, ignoring the elf's raised eyebrows at her cranky expression, then turned toward Dane, plastering on a smile.

God, he looked good up close. She'd already forgotten about his strong, whiskered jaw, and the way his brown eyes settled on her as if she were the only thing in the entire world that he cared about. Her heart melted a little bit before she could remember that he was probably her enemy. She cleared her throat. "Dane. Hey. So nice to see you again." Fake small talk was so not her thing, and she saw from the suspicious look on elf #1's face that he didn't buy it. Or maybe, he just heard the strangled mix of terror and lust in her voice. That could be it as well.

Dane walked up, his shoulders even wider than the built-like-a-brick-wall elf's, and, sadly, his face was much less friendly than it had been only moments before. So, yeah, definitely no romantic sleigh ride offer pending. Sob.

"I'm glad I caught you," he said, his eyes studying her face with a level of interest that didn't feel nearly as flirtatious as it had been when she had been parked on his lap. He held up the photo. "You dropped this, and I thought it might be important."

Jaimi felt her cheeks heat up, and she snatched it from his

hand, trying to get it before Emily or the elves noticed. "Thanks—"

"Mom! That's our photo of—"

She slammed her hand over Emily's mouth and anchored her against her hip. "So, yes, we were just heading back to the hotel—"

"So soon?" Dane smiled at her, a smile that still made sparks salsa happily down her spine. God, he was handsome. How was it possible that every woman in Rogue Valley wasn't lined up behind him, trying to get close enough to fondle him illicitly? "I see you met Santa's elves. How are they doing? It's their first time."

Emily beamed at Dane, apparently as enamored by him as Jaimi was, without the "Oh, God, he's going to either expose me or charm me into taking off my pants," baggage to complicate things. "They wouldn't let me climb into the reindeer pen," Emily announced, "but then they gave me food for them, so it was cool."

Jaimi managed a smile. "Thanks for saving her from herself," she said to the elves, even as she began to edge away. "But we really must go—"

"Jaimi's new to town," Dane announced, moving in beside her, so she was basically penned between the three large men and the fence. What the hell? Was she imagining it, or had they somehow made a secret pact to trap her? "Maybe she could sit with you and your families at the concert?" he said to the elves. "I bet her daughter would love Ava."

"What?" Jaimi stopped trying to retreat, staring in confusion at Dane. She had been so certain he was mad at her, but if he was, why would he offer up some local hospitality for her and Em?

Elf #1 narrowed his eyes, clearly wondering the same thing. "Yeah, sure, we can make that happen."

"That's great." Dane's words sounded pleased, but there

was still an edge to his voice that made Jaimi shift restlessly. This was not the same friendly, flirty hottie who had rescued her. He was tenser now, watching her as if he wasn't sure whether he was going to have to whip out his gun and take her down. "Jaimi, these are the best guys in town, and they're like my brothers. Meet Zane and Steen Stockton. Zane and Steen, this is Jaimi Hamilton and her daughter."

He dropped the names like a freaking bomb and then waited, staring at her.

Zane and Steen? Jaimi froze, her face morphing into horrified stillness as her chest started to hammer in panic. Emily squawked in surprise, and Dane's eyebrows went up with expectation. *Holy crap.* He'd dropped that bomb to test her.

She had to pull out the deflection. She had to shrug it off, and play the "no big deal" card. Like *now.*

But no casual quip came to her mind. No clever response. Just absolute shock and numbness. She was rooted in place, frozen into paralysis, like an idiotic rabbit who thought that hiding in plain sight was a better response to an approaching coyote than actually…oh…maybe… *running like hell?*

She shot a panicked look at the elves, but from the mildly curious expressions on their faces, she knew they had no clue what was going on. They had no idea who she was, just as her mom had always told her. She was nothing to them. *Nothing.* For a split second, a huge crash of sadness pressed down upon her so hard she couldn't even breathe.

Dane frowned at her. "Are you okay?"

She shook her head once, unable to find her voice, unable to summon even a single word.

Emily tugged at her hand. "Mom?"

She couldn't even answer her daughter. She couldn't even fake a smile for her, which was astounding, given her expertise in faking it to keep Em happy.

Silence made time slow to a stop as the three men stared

at her, no doubt shocked by the look of absolute terror on her face. But she couldn't think of anything to say or do to break the moment. Her mind was an absolute blank.

Elf #1 (who was that? Zane? Steen?) glanced down at the photo in her hand, and his brow furrowed as he saw what was on it. When he looked back up at her, his eyes were narrowed. "What's that?"

At the sound of his voice, the deep tenor that was so different from Dane's, something snapped inside her, something she'd been holding taut her whole life. She looked back and forth between them, at Zane and Steen, in their elf hats. Which was which? She had no idea, but as she searched their faces, looking for some clue, the strangest feeling came over her.

These men were her brothers. Even if they had no idea who she was, *they were hers.*

Suddenly, tears filled her eyes, and her throat clogged. She stumbled backwards, her vision suddenly too blurry to see. "We have to go." The words were an unintelligible muddle, but who the hell cared at this point? Dignity was a lost cause, and escape was the only choice, no matter how klutzy, unprofessional, or pathetic it might be. "*Now*, Em."

For once, her daughter didn't argue. Emily gripped her hand tightly, and broke into a run to keep up as Jaimi practically sprinted across the festival grounds. Only once did Jaimi glance over her shoulder, and she saw the three men standing together, watching her.

They weren't talking.

They weren't looking at each other.

They weren't entertaining the kids.

They were completely, and entirely, focused on her.

She knew then that escape was only temporary. They were going to come find her. She had to get out of town, vacate before they found her, go back to Boston—

Her gaze settled on Dane, and her heart seemed to stop. She'd expected to see that same anger that had been on his face when he'd handed her the photo...except it wasn't there. There was no anger anymore. His jaw wasn't hard or flexed. The expression on his face...was concerned. Kind. Worried.

Surprised, she stopped running, staring across the crowds at him. Her chest hurt, either from the physical exertion, or from emotion, or from the fact that Dane was looking at her as if he wanted to hug her, not arrest her.

He said something to Steen and Zane, then detached himself from them and started walking toward her, not taking his gaze off hers. She tightened her hand around Emily's, unsure what to do. She wanted to run, to hide, to escape from this part of her life, to retreat back to the world that she knew...

But something kept her rooted in place. Something deeper. Something that was calling to her more deeply than the screaming of her inner wimp to run away.

"Are we going to introduce ourselves?" Emily whispered. "Or are we still spies?"

"I don't know," Jaimi whispered back. Dane was closer now, still watching her. His approach was different than it had been the last time. He was still in relentless pursuit, but there was a softness to his expression that made her heart ache. She had a sudden vision of falling into his arms and letting him envelop her in his protective strength.

God, what the hell? She didn't fall into anyone's arms. She was a badass single mom who karate-chopped men who tried to muscle their way into her precious mother-daughter circle.

"You don't know if we're spies?" Emily asked.

"I don't know what to do," she admitted. Her throat was dry now, and she knew she had to decide right then whether to walk away or let him catch up. She didn't feel like engaging in offensive martial arts with him. She wanted to stand there, like some pathetic lump, and let him sweep her off her feet like a fairytale prince who just happened to be wearing Wranglers, cowboy boots, and that calf-length jacket that was just so undeniably *male*.

Emily tightened her hand around hers. "I'm sorry I brought the photo," she whispered, her voice suddenly very small. "I didn't mean for them to see it."

Jaimi's heart squeezed, and she looked down at her daughter, at her worried little face, and the tears brimming in her eyes. "Oh, baby, it's okay." She crouched down and pulled Emily into her arms. "I love you."

Emily nodded, a single tear glistening on her cheeks. "I want a family," she whispered. "I really do. I want to tell them who we are."

Oh, God. How could she ignore that? Without Gram, it was just the two of them, alone in the entire damn world, and she knew Emily missed Gram more than she'd ever admit. Jaimi took a deep breath. "Gram always said everything happens for a reason, right?"

Emily bit her lower lip, her big blue eyes fixed on Jaimi. "Yeah."

Jaimi took another deep breath. God, she could barely breathe, her chest was so tight. "So, there must be a reason that the universe wanted Dane and the others to see the photo." *I can do this. I can do this. I can do this.* But she didn't feel like she could. But for her daughter, for her amazing daughter, she would try. She forced a strained smile. "So, let's see what that reason is, okay?"

"Really?" Emily stared at her, hope lighting up her face. "I thought we were running away."

Jaimi managed a laugh. "We were, but then I smacked down my inner wimp."

"Oh." Emily grinned. "Awesome."

"Yeah, awesome." Not quite feeling the vibe of "awesome," Jaimi lifted Emily onto her hip and then turned toward the men she'd left behind. Zane and Steen were still watching her, and Dane was only a short distance away.

She still had a second to flee, a second to retreat to her life.

Then Emily leaned her head against Jaimi's cheek, and resolution flooded her.

She had to at least try. She wasn't going to promise anything, even to herself, except that she wasn't going to run away this minute. For now, for this moment in time, she was going to stand right where she was and see what happened.

So, she tightened her grip on her daughter, lifted her chin, and waited for Dane to reach them.

CHAPTER 4

*D*ane had been sheriff for long enough that he pretty much always had his shit together. He knew what he needed to say, how he needed to say it, and what he wanted to happen.

But as he walked across the fairgrounds toward Jaimi and her daughter, he had no clue what he was going to say when he got there.

She had something going on with the men he considered his brothers, the men he'd give his life to protect. Zane and Steen had no idea who she was, or why she'd have all their names written down, but there had been no doubt that she'd known exactly who they were once he'd said their names.

He should have been ready to cart her off to jail to interrogate her. But when he'd seen the expression on her face, that look of absolute horror, mixed with indescribable anguish and longing, he'd suddenly decided that he'd been an absolute bastard to drop their names on her like that.

He generally considered himself a pretty good guy, so to feel like such an absolute thoughtless piece of shit was a new experience for him. He didn't care for it all that much, to be

27

honest. He liked being a good guy, and for her especially, that's what he wanted to be. But he also needed to protect the Stocktons. So...what the hell did he do next?

As he neared them, Jaimi stood taller, her arms tightening around her little girl, who was propped on her hip. Her daughter's arms were wrapped around Jaimi's neck, and she was resting her cheek against her mom's shoulder, both females watching him approach.

He realized they weren't going to try to run away. They were standing there, in the middle of the crowd, waiting for him. Waiting for *him.* Protectiveness surged through him like a fierce fire, and his jaw tightened. He was *not* a bastard. He was a ruthless cop when he needed to be, yeah, but never a bastard, and not to her.

He took a deep breath as he approached, caught in the power of their stares. The nervousness on Jaimi's face was apparent, and her daughter was watching him with wide eyes, wide blue eyes that... Dane frowned. Damn. Her daughter's eyes looked familiar as well. Who the hell was she?

He looked back and forth between them again. Jaimi's dark eyes were riveting, but it was her cheeks, jaw, and nose that looked familiar. For her daughter, it was those eyes. He absolutely knew them—

"Hi." Jaimi spoke first as he neared, and something inside him turned over at the sound of her voice. It was soft and throaty, a little on edge, a little cautious. Her lips were pale in the cold air, and her breath puffed in soft, white clouds.

She looked brave and vulnerable, and suddenly, he could think of nothing other than pulling her into his arms, folding her against him, and wrapping them both up in his strength.

Son of a bitch. He had to find out what was going on, and fast, because right now, she was a potential threat to his family, not a lost filly needing a home. He stopped in front of her. "You okay?"

Shit. That was his first question? Not a "what's up with you and my boys?" Not a "tell me what's going on?" What kind of sheriff was she turning him into?

She nodded once. "Yeah, fine."

Silence descended, and he knew she was waiting on him, waiting for him to start in on her, but he couldn't find the words. How could she be a threat? It made no sense, not with how he was responding to her. He'd been around. He knew bad people, and he'd know if she was a problem. But she was hiding things, things that involved people he cared about. He had to figure it out, and get it out of the way, so he could focus on her. "You want to talk about it?"

He blinked at his question. What the hell kind of interrogation was that? That was more like a touchy-feely bonding than a "I need an answer now, and you're going to tell me."

And, as he would have expected, she shook her head. "No."

Her daughter watched him. "Mom's afraid," she whispered to him, in a whisper that was pretty much a bellow. "Gram said we need to help her smack down her inner wimp—"

Jaimi covered her daughter's mouth with her hand. "Emily, shh, baby. Not now."

But Emily had said enough. Dane realized that Emily was right. There was fear in Jaimi's eyes, and also in her daughter's. He remembered all too well the days when his sister had had that same fear in her eyes, and he knew that the only thing either of them needed right now was a sense of safety. "It's okay," he said softly.

Jaimi shook her head. "You have no idea."

"I don't," he agreed. "But I have guns, fantastic aim, and an innate sense of responsibility, so you're in good hands."

She stared at him, and he knew she wasn't buying it...

which meant that she truly believed that she was hiding something that he wouldn't like.

Shit.

He had to find out what it was, and fast. Forcing it out of her wasn't the way. He just couldn't do that to her. Which meant he had to get them comfortable enough to volunteer the information... He glanced past them at the massive, puffy blue and red inflatable Santa's Village maze about a hundred yards away. "As sheriff, I get unlimited passes in the bouncy house." He looked at Emily. "You want to go in?"

A grin flashed across her face, a smile so electric that something inside him lit up. Shit. He had no idea that it could feel so good to make a kid smile. "Yes!" She looked at Jaimi. "Can we, Mom?"

Jaimi was staring at him, her brow furrowed in confusion. "I thought you were going to ask me about—"

"There's time." He held out his hand toward the bouncy house, inviting them. "Shall we?"

She still didn't move. "I can't—"

Dane swore under his breath and moved closer. "Jaimi," he said gently. "I can tell you're a good person. Whatever it is, it's okay. We'll work it out." He grinned. "Did I mention I'm the sheriff? I pretty much own this town. I'm all you need."

Tears suddenly swam in her eyes. "I can't do this," she whispered.

Emily wrapped her arms around her mom's neck, her face worried. "We're spies," she explained to Dane. "I don't want to be a spy, but mom says we have to be, until—"

"Shh." Dane put his finger over his lips. "Spies don't tell who they are, even to the sheriff. Top secret stuff is important."

Emily stared at him, then giggled. "You're nice. Are the Stocktons nice like you?"

Jaimi sucked in her breath. "Em—"

"Yes, they are." Dane didn't take his gaze off the little girl. "The Stocktons are a bunch of tough guys, but they have great hearts. Super nice. Some of them even have kids like you. They're great dads."

Emily looked up at her mom. "Did you hear that?"

Jaimi nodded, her brown eyes fixed on Dane's. "Really?" she whispered.

"Really." Dane noticed her shoulders relax ever so slightly, and some of the tension around her mouth faded. Satisfaction pulsed through him. He needed her to be okay. He needed both of them to be okay. And he needed to be the one to make them okay. "What do you say, Mom? A little bouncy house? I'll stand guard."

She managed a small smile. "Why are you being so nice?"

Dane gave her a lopsided grin and put on a cowboy drawl. "Well, ma'am, it's my sworn duty to take care of any unescorted women who arrive in this here town. I'll rustle up some grub for y'all, and you can bunk down in my homestead for as long as you need."

Emily giggled, and even Jaimi's smile widened to something almost real. "You're silly."

"Never. This here sheriff ain't got no time fer jokin'. Protecting wayward damsels is serious bizniss, ma'am." He took off his hat and held it over his heart. "First order of bizniss is to get a smile on that li'l filly's face. Time to head over yonder to that bouncy house, Miss Emily."

Emily burst out laughing, and even Jaimi chuckled. "Fine," Jaimi capitulated. "We'll go bounce." She glanced over his shoulder and he knew she was looking at the Stocktons one last time, before turning away.

Dane's feel-good moment from making them smile faded at the reminder that Jaimi and her daughter still carried secrets that he needed to solve. He swore under his breath.

As soon as Emily was in the bouncy house, he and Jaimi were going to talk.

He fell in beside them, and Jaimi glanced over at him. Some of the worry in her eyes was gone, and she gave him a small smile, so genuine, appreciative, and vulnerable that he wanted to beat his chest and do some testosterone male bellow, declaring that he would take care of her.

Since he didn't generally engage in chest beating, instead, he set his hand on her lower back. Her gaze shot to his as his hand made contact, and for a beat, he waited to see if she would move away from him. Then her smile widened, and she moved the tiniest bit closer to him, a move so imperceptible that he wouldn't have noticed if he weren't so focused on her.

But he *was* focused on her, and he did notice. So, he smiled back, let his hand rest more heavily against the small of her back, and wished it was a hell of a lot longer walk to the bouncy house.

CHAPTER 5

*J*aimi was so focused on Dane's hand on her back that she almost crashed into three different people on her way to the bouncy house. Three of them! And one of them was a huge guy who looked like he could carry an entire cow on his back, and yet she hadn't even noticed him until Dane had used his hand to shift her to the right at the last second.

Not that she hadn't liked his little "save the damsel" action. Maybe she'd subconsciously decided to endanger herself just so he could rescue her...nah, she wasn't that pathetic.

Or maybe she was. Because literally, all she could focus on was that pressure on the small of her back, and the way the back of her arm kept bumping his as they neared the bouncy house.

"Oh, Mom! It's *huge*. It's a complete maze." Emily wiggled to get free, and Jaimi reluctantly let her go.

Dane released Jaimi to escort Emily to the bouncy house, right to the front of the line. He chatted briefly with the attendant, then crouched down to talk to Emily. His face was level with hers, and he was speaking gently, his eyes twinkling with kindness as he spoke to her.

God, how nice was his manner with Emily? The guy was big, muscly, and strong, and yet he was like a massive, endearing bear hug. Emily nodded at whatever he said, and then the two of them quickly took off her boots and replaced them with what appeared to be warm, knit slippers that went halfway up her calves. His hands were gentle as he helped Emily change, and Emily rested her hands trustingly on his shoulders for balance. It was a sweet, endearing moment. Anyone watching them would have thought they were father and daughter, a moment that Emily had never experienced in her life, and one that Jaimi had never witnessed for her daughter.

It looked so perfect, so sweet, so natural...and was so not the life they really had. She had to remember that.

Emily darted up the ramp into the bouncy house, and Dane stood up. Jaimi's belly tightened as she watched his strong legs flex as he stood. He turned toward her, his gaze settling on her. Suddenly, all his "dadness" was gone, just *bam!* disappeared, and all that was left was pure unadulterated *male.*

Heat pulsed down her spine as he walked toward her, a slow, casual walk of athleticism and strength. She swallowed as he reached her. "Emily can stay on as long as she wants," he said with an unapologetic grin. "I completely took advantage of my position to clear the way for her."

"Thanks for looking out for her." He was so close that she had to look up at him. She hadn't realized how tall he was. She wasn't exactly short, but he was so utterly *male*...not to overuse that word a million times, but yes, she was going to overuse that word a million times because it fit him, and because she was so hyperaware of his maleness in a way she'd never been before, not with anyone.

"My pleasure." He gestured to the side, near a wooden post-and-rail fence. "If we sit here, we can see her most of the time, depending on where she is."

"Um, okay." Her heart started to pound as she walked past him and climbed up on the fence, sitting on the top rail, her feet braced on the middle rail. She almost wanted to hold her breath as Dane climbed up beside her, parking himself close enough that his shoulder brushed against hers.

Her heart leapt, but she didn't pull away, and neither did he. He was going to ask her about the Stocktons, and she didn't know what she was going to say. She didn't know how to handle it. She didn't know—

"Jaimi, it's okay. Relax." Dane leaned close to her, bumping his shoulder against hers. "I'm not your enemy, I swear. I want to find out what's going on so I can help you."

She bit her lip, her heart starting to race. How could she just tell him? Just announce that she had nine brothers she'd never met? Saying it out loud made it real, made it a fact she'd have to deal with, instead of pretending it wasn't real and shrinking back to her condo in Boston. If she told him, she was going to have to acknowledge it and make a decision on how to handle it.

"Hey." He slid his arm around her shoulders and squeezed. "It's okay. It really is."

She inhaled sharply, shocked by how amazing it felt to have his arm around her shoulders. God, she wanted to just close her eyes and lean into him, to concentrate on the weight of his arm across her shoulders, on the delicious sensation of his hand wrapped around her upper arm, holding just tightly enough to offer reassurance, and not tightly enough to feel like a threat. She hadn't been held by a man in so long, hadn't been touched in so long, she couldn't believe how her entire soul was crying out, wanting it, aching for more.

How could his touch feel this good, when she didn't even know him? Except she did know him, at least on some levels. He was strong. He was honorable. He was incredibly kind to her daughter. He loved the Stocktons deeply, a fact that was so evident in his tone when he'd been talking about them. He was funny. And he made her feel like a woman in a way that no one ever had before. With a sigh, she glanced at him. "How do you know it will be okay?"

"Because it always is," he said softly. "Regardless of what's bothering you, you're sitting here on the fence, safe and okay. Your daughter is safe and okay. I'm sitting next to you, and I'm born to protect. So, in this moment, in this exact second, everything is okay."

She raised her brows at him, surprised by his logic. "That's kind of simplistic."

"But true, right?"

She sighed, looking away from him to check on Emily. She had climbed to the top of a ramp, and as Jaimi watched, her daughter dove headfirst down the slide, bouncing and laughing as she tumbled with the other kids. "Yes, I guess it is."

They were quiet for a moment, and she became increasingly aware of the way their upper arms were pressed against each other. Her heart was racing, and she could feel her belly trembling. God, all this because he was a man? Or because he was a sheriff? Or the fact he was the Stocktons' good friend?

"Hey." He leaned closer, and she could feel the warmth of his breath against her ear.

She closed her eyes, concentrating on the sensation of his breath. God, it felt so intimate, and so good. "What?"

"If you won't tell me what you're hiding, at least tell me what potential repercussions are making you so damned scared?"

She opened her eyes and turned her head to look at him.

He was so close that her nose brushed his, but he didn't pull back.

Neither did she.

"I'm afraid of my world falling apart," she admitted quietly. "I'm afraid that everything I know will change, and I won't know who I am or what I'm supposed to do. I'm afraid of making a mistake that will destroy Emily's life, but I don't know which choice is the right one. I don't know what to do." She searched his face. "I'm afraid that the choice will be made for me, and I don't want that. I need to make the choice, but I'm scared as hell of making the wrong one, and terrified that even the right one might wreck my life, and—"

She stopped when he put his hand on her cheek. God, his touch was so soft. "What?" she whispered. "I should shut up?"

"Never." He brushed his thumb over her skin. "How can I help?"

She swallowed. "Don't ask me to tell you what's going on. I need time."

He paused for a moment, and a muscle ticked in his cheek. "I consider the Stocktons my brothers. I would protect them with my life." He searched her face, his gaze intense. "Do I need to protect them from you?"

Tears suddenly burned in her eyes. "They're so lucky they have you to protect them," she whispered. "It's so beautiful. A family like that. You're all so lucky—"

He put his thumb over her lips, silencing her. "Do I need to protect them from you?" he asked again, searching her face. "I need the truth."

She swallowed. Did he need to protect the Stocktons from her? God, it was so complicated. Maybe they did need to be protected from being saddled with a sister and a niece. Maybe she would ruin their lives if she admitted who she was. "I don't know," she finally said.

Dane sighed. "Are you planning to physically harm any of them?"

"No, God, no—"

"Are you planning to try to get your hands on any of their money?"

She laughed. "Honestly, Emily would, but I'm not. I can't promise anything on her behalf, but I don't want any money, or favors, or anything from them."

He cocked his head. "You know that statement makes it almost impossible for me not to ask what the hell is left that you would want them for, then."

She nodded. "I can imagine. I'm intriguing that way."

He chuckled "It's that cop thing. Makes me naturally inquisitive."

She eyed him. "It's not a cop thing. It's you."

He laughed softly, tugging lightly on a curl that had escaped from her hat. "Yes, this is true." His smile faded, and suddenly the tension between them curled tighter. "Here's the thing, Jaimi Hamilton. I've been looking for a woman for a long time, and I think you might be her."

Her heart suddenly started hammering. "You don't even know me—"

He put his thumb over her lips again, silencing her. "I'm not finished yet, sweetheart," he said, his eyes twinkling. "I'm attempting emotional intimacy, but I'm a guy, so I'm pretty sucky at it. If you interrupt me, it may never happen again."

Oh, God. Emotional intimacy. "I suck at it, too," she whispered. "I don't even know how to date."

"I do. I've dated a shit ton. I got that covered for both of us." He leaned closer, so close she felt the warmth of his breath on her lips. "Here's my conflict. I'm interested as hell in you, and I'm feeling conflicted because I don't know if you're a danger to my boys. I can't make a move on you until

I know for sure you're no danger to them. So, do I kiss you, or arrest you? What do you think?"

"Kiss me?" she echoed, her belly jumping. "You want to kiss me?"

"Yeah." He slid his hand behind her neck. "I also want to protect you, to make you and that cute kid of yours feel safe, and I want to help you with whatever's bugging you. That's what I want."

Her throat tightened. "You are way too nice of a man to be sniffing around me. I'm incapable of a relationship."

"Are you?" He leaned closer, and lightly pressed a kiss against the corner of her mouth.

Oh, *God.* She thought she might melt right then. "Yes," she whispered. "I'm paranoid about bringing a man into my life who might upset our little family. I chase them off every time anyone gets close. I was thinking of buying pepper spray to make sure men stay away from me."

He pressed a light kiss to the other corner of her mouth. "I have pepper spray. I can keep you supplied. I'm helpful like that."

Oh, God. "Don't want me, Dane. I can't handle it. And I'm going back to Boston after Christmas."

"It's okay if you can't handle it, or can't figure it out. I'll do the hard parts. I'm great at holding shit together." He cupped her chin. "Just look me in the eye and tell me that you aren't here to cause trouble for the Stocktons."

She met his gaze. God, he was intense. And handsome. And completely serious. "I'm definitely not here with the goal of causing trouble for them." Which was the truth, the absolute truth.

He grinned, his face lighting up, making him look so much younger than he had a moment ago, almost like a mischievous teenager. "I believe you. You're extremely earnest."

She gave a nervous laugh. "I'm a school teacher. We're all highly moral. It's required."

"Kind of like cops. We're all good guys."

She laughed again. "All of you?"

"Yeah." His smile faded. "Since I believe you, that means I'm not going to have to arrest you. So, you know what that means?"

She swallowed. "What?"

"It means that I have to go with option two. You remember what that is?"

Oh, *God.* "That you need to kiss me?"

He grinned. "That I need to kiss you." He bent his head toward her, leaning closer, his hand tightening around the back of her neck, drawing her closer to him. "You okay with that?"

She swallowed. "I told you I don't know how to date. I'm going back to Boston in a few days. I'm a man-hating single mom and—"

He kissed her.

CHAPTER 6

*T*he moment Dane felt Jaimi's lips against his, he knew he'd been right. It was right. *She* was right. Not to be melodramatic, but he was pretty sure he'd finally found what he'd been searching for his entire life. The kiss was more than magic. It was the awakening of his soul, the settling of a deep, penetrating peace throughout every inch of his body. It was a realization that he was exactly where he was supposed to be: with her, on that fence, three days before Christmas.

She made a soft sound against his lips, a sound that made a sense of absolute protectiveness and possessiveness rush through him. He slid his fingers beneath her hat, into the tight curls at the nape of her neck, angling his head as he deepened the kiss. Not too much. Just enough to taste her, to claim her, to make promises he knew she wasn't ready to accept.

The woman who purported to need pepper spray to keep him away didn't pull back. In fact, her hand went to his chest, resting just over his heart, as she kissed him back, a tentative, beautiful exploration that made his own chest tighten. What male wouldn't want to go all he-man when a woman like Jaimi decided he was worth kissing? He already knew the woman was special.

He paused in the middle of the kiss, his entire body needed to bask in the sensation of her hand against him. Such a tiny action, and yet such a significant one, one that felt better than a fast gallop on a great horse at dawn, and he sure as hell loved his dawn rides.

She hesitated, her lips stilling against his, drawing his focus back to the off-the-charts incredible sensation of her lips against his. He pulled back just enough to nip at her lower lip, eliciting a little smile from her, then kissed her again, a delicious, leisurely exploration of lips and tongues, a flirty but sensual dance unlike anything he'd ever experienced.

Not that he was the kind of guy who had kissed his way through a string of women, but he was no innocent newbie when it came to kissing. He knew when a kiss was good, and he knew when it was the best damn kiss he'd ever had. This kiss with Jaimi didn't simply fall into the latter category, it *owned* it. Best damn kiss ever, with no chance of being dethroned.

As if she'd heard his thoughts and decided to give him the answer to his prayers, Jaimi curled her fingers into the front of his jacket, gripping tightly, holding him closer, kissing him deeper—

"Mom! Dane!"

Dane swore and jerked back as a small hand grabbed his pants leg. He looked down to see Emily standing in front of them, staring up at them expectantly.

As much as his heart had responded to Jaimi's kiss, seeing that little face gazing up at him made something shift inside him. Something deep inside him that was both soft and fiercely protective.

Keeping one hand on Jaimi's arm to make sure she didn't lose her balance, he immediately hopped down, and knelt in front of Emily. "What's wrong?"

"You have to come!" Emily said.

"Come where?"

Jaimi shifted, and he looked up to see her starting to climb down. He immediately held his hand out to her to offer assistance. She glanced at his hand, then her gaze flicked to his. There was a moment of hesitation in her eyes, then she shook her head. "I'm all set." Leaving his hand suspended in the air as she jumped down and knelt in front of her daughter. "Hey, baby cakes. What's up?" She didn't even look at Dane, and her cheeks were pink.

He swore under his breath as he lowered his hand. Her message had been clear. The kiss had been spontaneous, but she was now pulling back, hard and fast. He couldn't shake the feeling of disappointment, but at the same time, he knew he should've been expecting it.

She'd already warned him that she wasn't interested in anything that led to holding hands or anything romantic like that. She'd made sure he knew that she didn't allow men into her circle with her daughter.

It was a smart strategy. Most men were bastards who wouldn't be worthy of being a part of the brilliant bond that the two of them had. As he watched Jaimi crouched in front of her daughter, he knew that he couldn't fuck around with them. If he inserted himself into their circle, even a little bit, he had to mean it. He had to be committed to staying there, and being worthy of their faith.

Was he willing to go all in with a duo he'd just met? Was he willing to say "yeah, I'm in," when he didn't even know what Emily's favorite color was, or what Jaimi's favorite dessert was, or what were their greatest fears, or their biggest dreams. He didn't know any of that, and at this point, he didn't deserve to, not until he could promise them and himself that they could trust him with every inch that they gave him of their faith and their hearts.

These two were playing for keeps. He had to do the same if he decided to go forward. It wasn't just about a kiss. It was the whole nine yards. Was he prepared for that?

Emily looked up at Dane, ignoring her mom. "They're closing the bouncy house for the night. The man said that I could stay if you went in with me. Will you go in with me, Dane?" She belatedly glanced at Jaimi. "And you, too, but Dane has to stay, 'cause he's the sheriff."

Jaimi glanced up at him. "I think we need to go find our hotel, check in, and get some warmer clothes. I'm sure Dane has sheriff stuff he needs to do."

He met her gaze, and he saw her intention. He'd passed her comfort zone, and she was retreating as fast as she could. She wasn't simply giving him an out if he wanted to take it. She was putting up a wall between them that she planned to reinforce with some solid steel plates the moment he turned his back. If he let her get away now, she'd have her shields back up so fast that he might never get through them again.

But if he stayed, he had to mean it. He had to mean it in the big, long-term way. A guy didn't fuck with a single mom and her kid, especially not these two. He looked back and forth between them, at Jaimi with her emotional guards, and big brown eyes. At Emily, with her big blue eyes that were so familiar, at the hope in them.

He knew. He didn't have to ask himself. No deep questions. He'd been around enough and been through enough to know what he wanted. He wanted them. Not just Jaimi. He wanted the whole package, and he knew it. He also knew it would be a hell of a battle to get them to trust him, but that didn't matter. He knew what he wanted. "I can stay for a few minutes," he said, barely hiding a grin at Jaimi's look of dismay.

"Yay!" Emily launched herself at him, and he barely got his arms up in time to catch her in a hug. "Thanks, Dane! You're the best!" She whirled toward her mom and grabbed her arm. "Come on, Mom! Let's go!" She took off toward the bouncy house, and sprinted up the ramp, bouncing and laughing as she scurried out of sight.

Jaimi put her hands on her hips and turned toward Dane. "You're a pain in the ass."

He grinned. "Yeah, true. Want to go jump around?"

She didn't move. "Seriously. Did you not read my body language that I was trying to pretend that kiss had never happened? And I think I was pretty obvious when I told Em that you had sheriff stuff to do. Do I need to tattoo a sign on my head making it clear?"

He grinned and walked over to her. "Sweetheart, are you telling me that you didn't like that kiss? Not even a little bit?"

She narrowed her eyes. "Maybe a little, but that doesn't mean I want to acknowledge it actually happened. Denial and avoidance are sometimes a woman's best friend, and I'm pretty sure now is one of those times."

"You liked that kiss only a little? I'm devastated." Ignoring everything past that ego-crushing acknowledgment, Dane cupped her chin. "I strive for much higher standards than that. I gotta prove you wrong. Let me have another crack at wowing you." Before she could protest, he caught her mouth in another kiss. This time, he didn't keep it gentle. He went all-in, and it took only about three seconds before she sighed and slid her arms around his neck.

"Daaane!" Emily shouted. "You have to get in here!"

He finished the kiss with a few teasing pecks, then pulled back, grinning at the dreamy expression on Jaimi's face. "Damn, you're beautiful."

She blinked, and he saw her summon herself back into her tight, protected emotional ball. "You are a dangerous man."

"Thanks. I'll take that as a high compliment." As he spoke Emily bellowed for him again. "Coming, Em!" Grinning, he left Jaimi standing there as he jogged across the snowy ground to the bouncy house.

The woman moved fast, though, and by the time he got his boots off and was in his socks, Jaimi had caught up to him. "Dane!"

He glanced at her, then stopped when he saw the tension in her face. Shit. He hadn't intended to push her to the point of angst. "What?"

"You know how I said that I wasn't here with the goal of causing trouble for the Stocktons?"

He frowned. "Yeah?" Was this another attempt to drive a wedge between them? He knew it probably was, but he couldn't keep his internal alarms from going off. The Stocktons were the only family he had, and he would protect them with his life. Jaimi knew that, and she was playing that card. He had to stay focused and see through it.

"Well, that's true. I'm not here for the *purpose* of causing trouble for them." She set her hands on her hips. "But the truth is that my very existence might cause a major shitload of trouble for them. And it might cost them money, though it's not my intention. This kind of thing has a way of getting way out of hand, and I can't promise it won't. So, think on that before you kiss me again." Then she handed him the photograph of Chase, the ones with all the names on it. "My mom always taught me that my biggest goal in life should be to cause trouble, and I have always tried to be a good daughter."

Then, without another word, she kicked off her boots,

and vaulted up the ramp of the bouncy house, leaving Dane staring after her.

Son of a bitch.

He'd seen the look in her eyes. She was dead serious. *Shit.* He knew she hadn't fabricated that speech simply to get him to back off. She'd meant it.

What in the hell was going on with her?

"Dane!" Emily grabbed the netting from the second level of the bouncy house and peered down at him. "You have to be inside the bouncy house! Come on!"

Shit. There was no more time to be flirty with Jaimi. She'd laid down the gauntlet, and she'd underestimated how important the Stocktons were to him. He was getting the answers, and getting them now.

No matter what it took.

Yeah, he needed to kiss her. Again, and again. But his first priority was the Stocktons. It had to be.

Screw the kisses. This was about family now. His family. He clenched his jaw and headed up the ramp—

Then his phone rang. The ring for his sister. Swearing, he paused and grabbed his phone out of his pocket. "Zoey? You okay?"

"I'm coming home, Dane."

Dane sank down onto the ramp, pressing his hand to his forehead. "Don't say that, sis. You can get through this. I'll help—"

"No. It's over. I'm not doing it anymore. I'm coming home."

"No." His hand tightened on the phone. "Don't give up on this. You deserve it—"

"It's not my dream anymore. I'm over it. I'm coming back. I'm too tired to fight it anymore. Just let it go. Support me. I'll be home by the end of the month."

He bowed his head, defeat settling deep inside him. "Can

you at least think it over? Give it another week. No decisions yet."

"Dane—"

"What's a week? You lose nothing. Take a week. Don't make the same mistake Dad did."

She sighed. "You're a complete ass as a brother sometimes."

He grinned, recognizing her capitulation. "You love me."

"Yes, but sometimes I want to strangle you." She sighed. "Fine, I'll wait a week. But I'm not going to change my mind, and in a week, you have to support my decision, or I'll hunt you down and shave your head while you sleep."

He grinned at the threat she'd made so many times when they were kids. "Deal." His smile faded. "How can I help?"

She was quiet for a moment. "There's nothing you can do, but thanks. I have to go. I'll talk later."

"Yeah, okay. Be safe." Dane hung up the phone, and sighed. He was completely helpless to protect his sister, and he hated that. He'd spent his entire life trying to protect those he cared about, and there wasn't a damn thing he could do right now. Fuck. He hated feeling so incapable of protecting those who mattered to him.

"Dane!" Emily shouted for him, and he looked up at the little girl waving at him. Jaimi quickly pulled her back from the screen, but not before Dane saw the wary look on her face.

Resolution flooded him. He might not be able to do a damned thing to help his sister right now, but he could protect the Stocktons by finding out what the hell Jaimi was hiding.

He stood up and shoved the phone in his pocket. "I'm on my way, Emily."

Hell, yeah. He was on his way.

CHAPTER 7

*J*aimi tensed when she saw Dane racing up the ramp into the bouncy house. He'd left his jacket outside, and was wearing jeans, heavy socks, and a heavy sweatshirt that made his shoulders and arms look incredibly muscular.

Dammit.

She did not want to be noticing him! She pulled back from the netting she'd been using to spy through (What? Spying on a guy? Her? Never.) and turned toward her daughter. "Are you getting hungry? We should go get dinner, huh? We really need to check into the hotel. Don't you want to see our room?"

"Nope!" In a blanket rejection of every escape route Jaimi could conceive of, Emily leaped backward, landing butt first on the green fabric. "Come on, Mom! Jump!"

Jump.

Yeah, she'd like to jump.

Like out of the bouncy house, into a snowbank, and run for her life.

Or, conversely, she'd like to jump right into Dane's arms

for another one of those incredible, soul-melting kisses. Yes, she knew she'd done a fantastic job rejecting him with her one-two hit of not taking his oh-so-tempting outstretched hand, which had so not been easy, and then basically threatening his family (God, had she really done that?), but the truth was that she'd come on hard and fast in her rejection of him because she had liked that kiss and being in his arms so damn much.

Like *so* damn much.

And when she'd seen the way he'd leapt off the fence literally the *instant* that Emily had called for help, her heart had done all sorts of funny things. She'd even imagined for a moment how lucky Emily would be to have a dad like that, one who was so attuned to her that one little shout for help would instantly break through a kiss-induced-haze. She was pretty sure she'd just lost a few points on the good-mom-scale after being so entranced by the kiss that she hadn't even heard Emily's demand for attention until after Dane had already vaulted heroically to the ground.

Granted, she had a highly-tuned-mom-radar, and she was sure she'd instantly recognized the demand as one that didn't involve blood, danger, or serious bodily harm, but *still*. It would have been good if she'd at least *heard* it, right? But she hadn't. Because she had been absolutely consumed by the kiss with Dane.

She'd been kissed plenty of times in her life, but none of them had ever affected her like Dane's. His kiss had been deeply sensual, incredibly tender, and utterly captivating. Every intention she'd had to keep him at a distance had vanished the moment that he bent his head and kissed her. And now, despite her best efforts to reclaim her status as an independent, man-hating, solitary, completely happy with herself, single mom, she could not keep from adding "completely melted over a certain sheriff" to her list of attributes.

The cauldron of heated masculinity and kindness drew her attention as he jogged effortlessly through the maze toward the main part of the bouncy house, where she and Emily were. She grimaced as she watched him approach.

How on earth could she maintain the illusion that she wasn't hopelessly drawn to him whenever his lips were anywhere near hers? And what about when he was jumping around next to her, and most likely bumping into her as they fought for balance in that space that was built for small children with no sense of personal space, not two adults who knew what each other's tongues tasted like? Seriously. She was incredibly well disciplined, but some things were beyond even her capacity.

Despite her neurotic single-mom-need to make up for the lack of a traditional family by overindulging her daughter's every whim and desire, it was time to abort the bouncy house. "Okay, Em. Five minutes and then we go, okay?"

"Okay!" Emily stood up and bent her knees, clenching her fists by her side. "Ready, Mom! Jump!"

Determined to be completely immersed in playtime with her daughter so that she would have an excuse not to notice Dane (as if!) when he got there, Jaimi jumped forward, landing just in front of her daughter. Her landing sent Emily shooting into the air, amid shrieks of laughter. Despite her kiss-induced angst, Jaimi couldn't help but laugh as her daughter tumbled.

Just as she started to relax and forgot to be super stressed and anxiety-ridden, Dane appeared at the entrance to the maze. She had no time to freak out before he leapt out beside her, landing so hard that she shot into the air. She shrieked as she tried to catch her balance, waving her arms like a freaking lunatic as Emily burst into hysterical laughter. Failing utterly to maintain any sense of decorum, she landed right on her butt and tumbled into the netting.

"Yes! That was a great one, Dane!" Emily jumped and landed beside her, upending Jaimi into a somersault that left her wedged in the crevice between the netting and the floor. "Go Mom!"

Dane appeared beside her and held out his hand, grinning. "Come on, sweetheart. Let's give this kid a ride."

There was literally no way for her to extricate herself without Dane's help, so Jaimi took his hand. Sparks flew, naturally, because it would have been way too convenient to no longer be attracted to him, but the moment he had her on her feet, instead of sweeping her up into another soul-melting kiss, he jumped, shooting both her and Emily into the air.

Emily's gales of laughter were so jubilant, that Jaimi couldn't help but burst out laughing. Oh, hell. Who had time to be miserable? Life was too short.

"Let's get Dane," Emily yelled. "On three!" She grabbed Jaimi's hand, and they both turned on Dane, who was faking terror and stumbling backwards. "Now, Mom!"

They both jumped, and their landing popped Dane off his feet, launching him sideways into the wall. He was back up almost instantly, a huge grin lighting up his face, making him look so appealing that Jaimi wanted to run away screaming, and simultaneously grab his shoulders, body slam him to the bouncy house floor, and pin him there with her breasts in his face.

Or just get a third kiss. Either of the latter two options worked for her.

Due to Emily's sex-neutralizing-presence, however, she went with option number four, and bounced Dane off his feet just as he was regaining them. Emily was shrieking with laughter, and when Dane went after her and bounced her off her feet, Jaimi couldn't help but laugh along with them.

Within moments, the bouncy house became a shrieking

festival of laughter, klutziness, and ruthless assaults. Dane was hilarious, making both of them laugh so hard that she gave up trying to keep her shields up. There was no way for her to be upset when her daughter was so happy, and Dane was the cause of that.

For now, she was just going to laugh, and enjoy the most fun she'd had in a very, very long time.

~

"IF YOU'D ASKED me an hour ago if I was in good shape, I'd have said hell, yeah." Dane groaned as he stretched out on his back in the bouncy house, his quads burning. "Apparently, the correct answer is actually that I'm a middle-aged couch potato, going on elderly."

Jaimi was stretched out beside him, breathing hard. "I was pretty sure I was way out of shape, and now I'm convinced," she said with a laugh. "But that was hilarious!"

"Come on, you guys!" Emily pounced between them, making both of them groan. "You can't stop!!"

Dane grinned. "No chance, kiddo. You outlasted us both." He couldn't remember the last time he'd had so much damn fun. He'd come into the bouncy house ready to confront Jaimi, but when he'd walked in and seen them jumping, and heard their laughter, all he'd wanted was to join in.

And it had been the best hour of his life...but as he lay there, catching his breath, his good mood began to fade as reality set in. He still had to deal with the secrets Jaimi was hiding—

"Dane!" Emily crawled over to him and leaned over his face, staring down at him. Her face was about six inches from his, her bright blue eyes glistening with amusement.

He grinned up at her. How many times had he seen that same look on Chase's face when they were kids? That look that he was up to no damn good and was damn pleased about it—

Chase. Emily's eyes reminded him of Chase's... Holy fuck. Shock ripped through him.

He looked at Emily again, at those blue eyes of hers and he knew. Son of a bitch. She had the Stockton eyes. What the bloody hell? Had Jaimi slept with one of the Stocktons? Was Emily the daughter of one of them? Anguish ripped through him, a violent, brutal anguish. *Did Jaimi belong to one of the Stocktons?*

Suddenly unable to breathe, he scrambled to his feet, stumbling backward. He would never touch Jaimi if one of the Stocktons had a claim on her. Never. Ever. He'd never cross that line, but son of a bitch. She was the one he'd been looking for...and she belonged to one of them?

Jaimi sat up, propping herself on her elbows. "Dane? Are you all right?"

He shook his head. No. He had to be wrong. He looked at Emily again, at those big blue eyes...and there was no way to lie to himself. She had Stockton eyes. How had he not noticed before? How in the bloody hell had he not realized it the first second he'd looked at her?

He looked at Jaimi, frowning at him. A thousand questions were spinning in his head. A thousand fucking questions. He didn't even know where to start... He thought of the names on that photograph. She'd listed *all* the brothers. Why all of them? Why not just the one who'd fathered her daughter?

She'd had Chase's photo.

Chase's.

Chase was Emily's dad? *Jesus.* Chase had a wife and a kid now. Did Jaimi know that? How long ago had it happened? "How old are you, Emily?"

"Six and three quarters."

Six years. Before Mira and J.J. But still…

Jaimi sat up. "What's wrong?"

He looked at her. "I recognize her eyes."

Jaimi gazed at him blankly. "Whose eyes?"

"Emily's."

Jaimi still looked confused. "What do you mean?"

He stared at her, suddenly equally confused. How would she not know what Chase's eyes looked like? "She has the Stockton eyes. Like Chase." *Like Chase.* A sudden burst of anger and resentment rushed through him, shocking him. Hell. He wanted to track Chase down and punch the bastard's lights out. Yeah, granted, he'd done that plenty of times as kids, but that had been for fun, not for real. Right now, he felt like he hated the guy. Chase had slept with Jaimi. He had a kid with her. *Son of a bitch.*

Shock filled her face. "What?"

"What?" Emily grabbed his arm. "My eyes are like Chase's? Really? His are blue, too?" She spun around. "Mom! Did you hear that! I have the same eyes as Chase! He'll believe us, now, won't he?"

Jaimi didn't take her gaze off him, but he could see the terror in her eyes.

He didn't know what to say.

She didn't respond.

Only Emily talked, rattling on excitedly, talking about family and the ranch and becoming a barrel racer, while Dane stood there, feeling like his world was falling away from him.

CHAPTER 8

*J*aimi felt frozen, her heart stuttering in her chest. The shock and accusation in Dane's eyes was brutal, tearing away at her.

He knew.

He'd figured it out. Emily's eyes had given away their secrets. He knew they were Stocktons.

She had no idea that Emily's eyes were recognizable. Her mom had never told her. She must have known all along that if one of the Stocktons met Emily, they'd recognize her, taking away Jaimi's choices. No wonder she hadn't asked Jaimi to promise she'd introduce herself. She'd known that all she had to do was get them both out to Rogue Valley.

Damn you, Mom. Damn you for all your secrets!

Emily kept jabbering, pestering Dane with questions about the Stocktons, but he didn't seem to hear her. He was just staring at Jaimi with a look of absolute shock and anguish on his face.

It was the anguish that got to her. Why was he so upset? Was she so awful? Was it that devastating that she was related to the men he considered his family? Tears suddenly clogged her throat, and she stumbled to her feet. "Damn you, Dane! That's not fair!"

"What's not fair?" His voice was hard. Cold. Rough.

"Looking at me like that! Emily and I are amazing, and anyone would be lucky to have us as family!"

More anguish crossed his face, so devastating that she almost started crying. "Don't look at me like that," she whispered. "It's really rude."

"Rude?" He blinked. "*Rude?*"

"Yes, rude!" She almost shouted the words. "You kissed me an hour ago, and told me how great I was, and now you're looking at me like it's the worst thing in the entire world that we're related to them!"

His brow furrowed, and he held up his hand. "What did you just say?"

"I said it's not the worst thing in the entire world to be related to us! And, personally, I find it really rude when you can say all these nice things to me an hour ago, and now you're looking at me like I have cooties or something!"

He blinked. "Cooties?"

"It's like boy germs, only worse," Emily explained. "We don't have cooties!"

He glanced at Emily, and then back at Jaimi. "*Us?* The Stocktons are *related* to *both* of you?"

She frowned at him. "What?" Crap. Had he *not* actually figured it out?

He walked toward her, his lithe body undulating as he made his way across the bouncy house floor. "*Us.* You said the Stocktons were related to *us.* What do you mean by that?"

Oh...shit. He *hadn't* figured it out. "Nothing. Emily, time to go—"

Before she could take even a step, Dane blocked her path with his body. She looked up, grimacing as she met his gaze. "Dane—"

"Did you sleep with Chase?"

"What?" She stepped back, horrified. "Of course not. That's disgusting."

Suddenly, the tension seemed to drain from his face. "Disgusting," he echoed softly. "Chase is a good-looking guy, and yet you think it would be disgusting to sleep with him."

"Of course I do, he's my—" Suddenly, Jaimi realized what was happening, what he thought. Her mouth dropped open. "You think I slept with Chase? That he's Emily's dad? That I—"

"No, I don't." Dane caught her chin and gently turned her head to the left. "I understand now," he said softly, his thumb rubbing gently along her jaw. "I know why you looked so familiar."

Oh. God. Her stomach dropped, and she looked at him. "Dane, don't—"

"You don't have the blue eyes, but you have the same facial structure." His face was softer now, gentle. "I can't believe I didn't see it."

She looked at him, begging him not to go there, not to open that door. "Dane—"

But he did. "You're a Stockton. Son of a bitch. You're their *sister*."

CHAPTER 9

*D*ane didn't need to see Jaimi's face to know that he was correct.

He had no doubt that he was.

Jaimi had the same piece of shit bastard father that the rest of the Stocktons had, but somehow, she'd escaped their childhood. She'd escaped their life...mercifully, beautifully, thankfully, she had escaped being raised by the bastard who'd fathered her.

He didn't know who her mother was, but she'd done damn well for herself, getting out of town before the old man had known about Jaimi. A cold chill clamped around his gut at the thought of what would have happened to Jaimi if she'd been raised in that home, about the lifelong scars she would have carried on her body and her soul if she hadn't escaped before he'd known about her.

His throat suddenly tightened, and he wanted to wrap her up in his arms and hug her, holding her tight so that the brutality of the life she might have led could never reach her. He even started to reach for her, unable to stop himself...

until he saw the look of absolute vulnerability and fear on her face.

She was terrified that he'd found out the truth...but why?

"Mom!" Emily grabbed Jaimi's hand. "Since Dane guessed, we don't need to be spies anymore, do we? We can tell them the truth, right?"

Jaimi didn't answer. She just stared at Dane. "Are you going to tell them?"

His first instinct was a *hell, yes*, but the words died in his throat at the expression on her face. "You don't want me to?"

She shook her head, lifting her hand to run it through Emily's hair. As she made the move, he noticed that her hand was trembling. Protectiveness surged through him, and he instinctively reached out and brushed a stray curl back from her face. "Why not?" he asked gently.

"I don't know if I want to tell them."

Resistance surged through Dane. "Family's the keystone to life. They would want to know you. You need them."

She shook her head. "No." Her voice was trembling. "I have all the family I need. I didn't know they even existed until two weeks ago. We've been just fine without them. I promised my mom I'd come out here, but I didn't promise I'd introduce myself." She gestured vaguely in the direction of the festival. "This isn't my world. I don't know them. I don't know if they'd want to meet me, and I don't know if I want to open that door. I didn't come here to meet them. I came here because it was the one thing my mom asked of me before she died. I—"

"Jaimi." He gently cut her off, his heart aching at her panicked rant. "I won't tell them." He made the promise before he'd even decided, and instantly regretted it. Not because he didn't want to support her, but because he'd meant it when he said family was what mattered. The Stocktons were his family, in every way that mattered, and he'd just sworn his loyalty to Jaimi instead.

Shit.

He owed them. There was no way he could keep that secret from them. They had a fucking *sister*. He almost laughed at what their reactions would be. They'd be so damned overprotective that she wouldn't know what hit her. They needed to know. They needed her. He looked at the two faces staring at him. Emily so happy and hopeful, Jaimi so worried, both of them waiting.

They needed the Stocktons.

"Thank you for not telling them," Jaimi said, relief evident on her face. "I appreciate it."

Shit. He'd made a promise. He never broke his promises.

Which meant he'd have to get her to make the choice herself to tell them...but even as he thought it, he realized that once the Stocktons knew about Jaimi, his problems were just beginning.

He was pretty damn sure that they knew far too much about his sordid past to ever let him date their sister...let alone the whole nine yards...which is what he wanted.

He wanted to go all the damn way with Jaimi and Emily.

Jaimi looked at him. "So, what now?"

What now? What now, indeed? He knew he had to find a way to bring her together with her family...and to win over her heart in the process...two almost impossible goals, given how damn tough and stubborn he already knew she was. He cocked his head, studying her, trying to assess the best way to handle it, to intrigue her. "Want to meet them?"

"Yes!" Emily screamed with delight. "Yes, please, please, please."

Uncertainty flickered across Jaimi's face. "Not yet. Can you let it go?"

He took a deep breath, knowing that the answer was no.

He also saw the vulnerability in her eyes, and he knew that if he pushed it, she would be on the next plane back to Boston. He knew, absolutely knew, that he couldn't let Jaimi and Emily walk out of town without meeting their family, and without following up on the connection he had with Jaimi. He also knew he couldn't allow them stay in town, keeping themselves isolated from him, and the family he knew would be dying to meet them. He had to find a way to bring it all together. "I'll make you a deal."

Jaimi gave him a wary look. "What's the deal?"

"I believe that you and Emily need to meet the Stocktons, and you need to tell them who you are."

Jaimi shook her head, a panicked look crossing her face. "No. You promised—"

"I promised I wouldn't tell them, and I won't break that promise." Unfortunately. "But I'll leave it alone and stop bugging you about it only on one condition."

She set her hands on her hips. "What?"

"That you go out to dinner with me tomorrow night, and we talk about it. I want to know your story, how you ended up in Boston, how you didn't know about the Stocktons until two weeks ago." His voice softened at the resistance on her face. "I already know the truth, Jaimi, the part you want most to keep hidden. Maybe it will help to talk about it." He grinned. "I'm a cop. I know how to keep secrets."

She wrinkled her nose at him. "You keep throwing around that 'I'm a cop' credential, like it makes you some great guy."

"No. I'm a great guy just 'cause I'm a great guy. But I'm throwing around the cop thing in case that helps you believe it." He looked at Emily. "What do you think?"

She gazed up at him. "I think my mom's inner wimp needs a smackdown."

He grinned at Jaimi. "See? We're all in agreement."

Jaimi looked at Emily, and then back at Dane. "What about Emily?"

"I can arrange a playdate for her."

"With—?"

He nodded, not offering it aloud, not wanting to step on Jaimi's toes in terms of parenting. He wasn't going to offer an evening with the Stocktons for Emily if Jaimi wasn't on board.

Jaimi sighed. "Can we do it tonight? I'll just dread it."

He nodded. "No problem. During the concert?"

She sighed again, but then she crouched down in front of Emily. "Hey, Em, I have a deal for you. Do you want to hang out with the…" She swallowed, and glanced at Dane before looking back at her daughter. "Do you want to hang out with the Stocktons during the Travis Turner concert while Dane and I grab dinner?"

Emily's jaw literally dropped open, and she got the most astonished look of awe on her face. She nodded once, apparently unable to actually talk.

Jaimi took her daughter's hands and squeezed them. "You have to absolutely promise not to tell them who we are. You can say your mommy is friends with Dane, and Dane thought that you would like to hang out with them while mommy and Dane went to dinner. Can you do that? It's very, very important to keep up being a spy right now."

Emily nodded solemnly. "I'm an amazing spy. I'm like a superhero. I can do anything."

Jaimi sighed. "Okay, then, but *promise*."

"I will!" Emily flung her arms around Jaimi, holding on so tight that she almost pulled Jaimi over. "Thanks, Mommy! Thank you so much! I love you so much!"

Tears filled Jaimi's eyes, and she hugged her daughter back. "I love you, too, sweet cakes."

As Dane stood there, watching the mother-daughter hug,

he realized why Jaimi had made that choice. Even if they never introduced themselves to the Stocktons, by letting her daughter spend the evening with them, she was giving Emily memories that would last her forever, memories that would make her feel anchored in this world for the rest of her life.

Jaimi Hamilton was a helluva mother, a helluva woman.

He wanted more than just the Stockton story at dinner tonight.

He wanted it all.

Every last bit.

But as she looked up at him, the wariness in her eyes, he knew she wanted to keep every last secret from him.

He smiled.

She hesitated, then smiled back.

And he knew he had a chance.

CHAPTER 10

*J*aimi shifted restlessly, holding Emily's hand tightly as Dane guided them through the crowd. People had thick blankets spread out on the snow, beach chairs, and there were portable heaters set up everywhere. There was a huge stage set up, and there were men and women in black jackets wandering around on it, making sure the equipment was in order.

For a town the size of Rogue Valley, she was surprised at how many people were present. Travis Turner apparently could draw crowds no matter how small the population was. There was smoke pouring into the air from the barbeque that was cranking out food for the crowd. She could smell the fire, and people were milling around, chatting happily.

It seemed like everyone knew each other. Wistfulness settled deep inside her, a yearning for a life where she felt so connected. She loved her small condo in Boston, but there was no sense of community like there was here. She nudged Dane. "Does everyone here know each other, or does it just seem like it?"

He smiled over at her. "Some of both. Folks come from all

over for this festival, but they usually come with family and friends, so there's a lot of connections between people."

She instinctively moved closer to him, her only anchor. She wasn't accustomed to being around so many people in such togetherness. She was used to being super tight with her mom and Emily, three generations of women sticking together and supporting each other, no matter what. This was different, and she didn't know how to fit in, or how to act, probably because none of them were her family or friends, and she felt weirdly isolated even though she was in a crowd.

She grabbed Emily's hand tighter, using Dane as her shield against her solitariness. Dane looked over at her, his eyes narrowed as he studied her face. Then he closed the distance between them, and set his hand on her lower back, just as he'd done before when they'd been walking toward the bouncy house. And, just like before, the mere feel of his hand on her back made her take a deep, shuddering breath as she felt her entire body settle.

There was something about being around Dane, about being connected with him, that made her feel grounded. Safe. Happy, even. She snuck a glance at him. He seemed to catch her movement, because he immediately turned his head to look at her, shooting her a genuine smile that made it impossible for her not to smile back.

She was still smiling when she turned her head back toward the crowd, then lost her smile when she saw a cluster of men, women, and kids camped out in the front row by the stage. She didn't have to ask. She knew instantly it was the Stocktons. Chase looked just like his picture, tall and strong, as he held a toddler and spoke to another man who looked similar to him.

Emily sucked in her breath and gripped Jaimi's hand. "It's

them," she whispered. "There are so many." She sounded awed, and a little afraid.

Jaimi stopped. "This is wrong. We can't do this."

Dane stepped in front of her, blocking her view of the Stocktons. "Hey, sweetheart, it's okay."

"It's not okay. Did you see Emily? She's afraid. This is wrong. I can't leave her with these strangers. We don't even know—"

"They're not strangers. They're your family."

Jaimi took a step back. "They aren't my family. Emily's my family. They are just strangers who we don't even know. Look at them! They all know each other! They spent their lives together! I'm just this shadow that exists on the periphery of their world that they don't even know about and don't need to know about. I—"

Dane set his hands on her cheeks, and her panicked words faded. "Hey," he said gently. "Take a deep breath."

God, his hands felt so good. Like amazingly good. Like, she wanted to melt into him and just let him be her strength.

"Breathe," he said again. "You can do it."

Jaimi did as he instructed, inhaling long and slow, trying to slow the pounding of her heart. "This doesn't feel right," she whispered.

He started to move his hands away, and she grabbed his wrist with her free hand. "No, not that. That feels great." He smiled and lightly traced his fingers along her jaw again. "Meeting them feels wrong. Leaving Emily with them. It doesn't feel right."

"Mom."

Jaimi took a deep breath and looked down at her daughter. "What's up, pumpkin?"

"I don't want to leave. I want to meet them." Emily stared up at her, with big blue eyes that were both afraid and vulnerable. "Don't make us leave."

Oh, God. Really, with the puppy dog eyes? "Do you do that on purpose? The puppy dog eyes?"

Emily nodded. "Is it working?"

Jaimi started laughing. "God, you're impossible."

Emily grinned. "That's what Gram says. She said I am supposed to say thank you when you say that."

"And that you should." Jaimi looked at Dane. "I can't do this alone," she whispered.

He nodded. "I've got you." He leaned forward and pressed a quick kiss to her lips, a kiss that was over before it started, and yet somehow managed to calm her down. Then he took her free hand and enveloped it in his warm, strong grip. "Let's go, ladies."

They headed forward again, one of Jaimi's hands held tightly by her daughter, and the other firmly ensconced in Dane's reassuring hand. As they got closer and closer to the Stocktons, she kept gripping his hand even more tightly. Her chest got tight, and she edged closer to Dane, so their shoulders were bumping. Emily moved closer to her as well, her steps getting smaller and smaller.

"Okay, hang on." Dane finally stopped and turned toward them. He held out his arms to Emily. "Come here, Em."

Relief flashed over Emily's face and she reached for Dane. He swept her up in his arms, tucking her against his hip as Jaimi had done so many times with Emily over the years. Then he slung his other arm around Jaimi's shoulder and pulled her against his side, nestling her snugly against him.

Instinctively, Jaimi slid her arm around his lean waist, locking them together.

He grinned at them both. "Good?"

They both nodded. Emily looked less nervous, and Jaimi definitely felt more secure. Maybe she didn't actually belong the way the rest of the people in the crowd did, but Dane certainly was a fixture here, and having him claim them made her feel secure. At least, secure enough that she didn't run screaming toward her rental car like a raving lunatic, which was always a good thing.

"Let's go, then." Dane started walking toward the Stocktons again, taking Emily and Jaimi with him.

Jaimi's tension mounted as they neared, but she kept her attention focused on the feel of Dane's body against hers, on the weight of his arm around her shoulders. Just as they were almost there, Chase noticed them. She tensed, half expecting this monumental, emotional moment, but her oldest brother simply raised his hand in casual greeting to Dane, nodded at her, and then turned to say something to one of his brothers.

She could not keep the disappointment from surging through her, but just as she felt her shoulders sag, Dane pulled her close and pressed a kiss to her cheek. "He doesn't know who you are," he said quietly. "If he did, you would already be wrapped up in a hug so tight you probably wouldn't be able to breathe for a week. You know that, right?"

She took a deep breath and nodded. "I know." She had known that even before Dane had reminded her, but just hearing him say it made her feel better. "Thank you."

He winked at her, and something inside her belly jumped. Then he nodded past her. "Ready?"

Oh, God. "No."

"Too late." He looked past her. "Chase. Hey. What's up?"

Jaimi sucked in her breath and turned her head to look in front of her. Chase, her brother, her *brother*, was walking toward them, still holding the toddler. His eyes were the same radiant blue as Emily's. For a moment, she started to panic, then Dane gave her shoulders a gentle squeeze, giving her the strength not to collapse into the snow on the spot. "Hey, Chase. I'd like you to meet Jaimi Hamilton and her daughter Emily. Ladies, please meet Chase and his son J.J."

Chase's son. That meant the little boy was her nephew. God. She had a nephew? Emily had a cousin? She hadn't thought of that, of more than brothers. Tears threatened again, and Dane began to play with her hair, a light reassuring touch that helped her regain control.

Chase nodded at them both. He gave Jaimi a curious look, his gaze going to Dane's arm wrapped tightly around her shoulders, before flicking back to her face. "Nice to meet you, Jaimi." He held out his hand, and Jaimi sort of felt like she was going to pass out as she reached out and shook the hand of her oldest brother, for the very first time in her life.

CHAPTER 11

"*N*ice to meet you, Chase." Jaimi's voice was hoarse, and she cleared her throat, trying to stay in control. "Thanks so much for being willing to watch Emily for a little bit."

Chase nodded, his gaze going right to the little girl. "Hey Emily," he said. "My name's Chase. How old are you?"

Emily silently held up six fingers.

"That's fantastic," Chase said. "My brother Maddox has a daughter named Ava who's going to be six in a couple months. She heard you're coming, and she's super excited to hang out with you. She claims she has too many boy cousins, and they're all going to be here tonight."

Emily leaned her head on Dane's shoulder, and watched Chase silently. Jaimi's heart tightened, and she elbowed Dane. "Maybe we shouldn't leave her here."

When she spoke, Chase looked over at her. He smiled gently, his blue eyes twinkling. "Don't worry," he said. "We're experts on kids over here. She'll have a great time."

Jaimi grimaced. She knew Emily's reluctance had nothing

to do with being shy, and everything to do with the fact that these people were her freaking *family.* "I don't think—"

"Hey, Jaimi." Another Stockton walked up and rested his forearm on Chase's shoulder. She recognized him immediately as one of the elves from earlier. He was the one with the earring, and now that he was out of his elf outfit, she could see that he did indeed match the biker persona. He was wearing a leather jacket, motorcycle boots, and jeans. He looked tough, and rough, and his eyes were assessing as he studied her. "Nice to see you again."

He was the one that had seen Chase's photo in her hand, with all the brothers' names on the back. It was clear from the expression on his face that he hadn't forgotten it, and he glanced at Dane with raised eyebrows, clearly asking what the situation was.

Dane squeezed her shoulders again, doing it with enough force to make it visible to the others that he was claiming her. Both brothers noticed, and they exchanged glances. "Jaimi," Dane said. "You remember Zane."

Zane. Another brother. She managed a smile. "Hi."

"Hey." He grinned at Emily as Chase turned away, giving a quick "I'll be right back," to Dane. "There's the little minx who tried to climb into the reindeer pen. You been causing more trouble since I saw you last?"

Emily giggled. "I'm trying."

Zane nodded approvingly. "That's my girl." He held up his hand. "High-five?"

Emily giggled again, and she let go of Dane with one hand so she could smack her little palm against Zane's.

"I hear you're going to hang out with us during the Travis Turner concert," he asked. "Is that right?"

Emily nodded again, smiling widely.

"What if I told you that we were about to head backstage to meet him? You want to come?"

Emily's jaw dropped open. "Really?" she gasped.

"Cowboy's honor." He held out his arms. "Maddox is already back there with Ava. She's stoked to hang out with you. You want me to take you back there?"

"Yes!" Emily grinned. "Mom! I'm going to meet Travis Turner."

Jaimi swallowed. "That's amazing."

Zane held up his arms. "You like shoulder rides?"

"Yes! My mom never gives them to me anymore because I'm too big!" Emily nearly flung herself out of Dane's arm, but Zane caught her easily and swung her up on his shoulders. She patted his cowboy hat excitedly. "Let's go, let's go!"

"Yes, ma'am." Zane shot Jaimi and Dane one more curious look, then turned and strode back toward the stage. As he walked, two boys joined him, both of them with skin about the same shade as Jaimi's, maybe a little lighter than hers, but close enough that she felt another tug of belonging. They were a mixed race extended family, one that she would fit into. Both boys were looking up at Zane as if he were the greatest thing ever.

"Those are his boys," Dane said. "He and his wife adopted them out of foster care last year. He's an incredible dad."

More cousins for Emily.

More nephews for her.

God, she felt like her head was going to explode, and she wasn't sure if it was in a good way or not, assuming that head explosions ever had a "good" way... "How many kids total?" she asked, her voice raw.

"Travis and Lissa have a daughter, plus Ava. So, six kids between all the Stocktons."

Six. *Six.*

Nine brothers. Six nieces and nephews. Plus sisters-in-law. "How many are married?"

"Chase is married to Mira." Dane pointed at a woman

sitting next to Chase, laughing as she bounced the toddler on her knee. "Maddox and his wife, Hannah are in back with Ava. That's Zane's wife, Taylor, sitting with Chase and Mira, in the red parka. Travis's wife, Lissa, is the one in the gray parka and red boots. Her daughter is probably backstage hanging with Travis as well. She still thinks it's super cool that her stepdad is Travis Turner—"

"What?" Jaimi gawked at Dane. "Travis Turner is Travis *Stockton*?"

He raised his brows in surprise. "You didn't know?"

"No, I…" She didn't know what to say. "I don't know anything about them," she said quietly.

"Well, let me finish intros, then." He pointed to another couple, who were setting up a space to eat on the thick blankets. "That's Steen, who you met, and his wife, Erin. They just announced that she's pregnant, so there will be at least one more Stockton by next summer." Steen looked up and saw Dane pointing. He nodded at them both, and then Erin looked up. She grinned at Dane and waved him over, but he shook his head. "Later," he called out. "We'll be back later!"

Dear God. "I have nine brothers, five sisters-in-law, six nieces and nephews, and one on the way." God, to say it aloud was overwhelming. She looked at Dane. "Two weeks ago, it was just me, my mom, and Em. Today…" She held out her hands, unable to find the words. Her throat ached with emotion, and she felt like she was going to cry.

He frowned and brushed her hair back from her face. "Let's get out of here, okay? Give you a break?"

She nodded, her chest so tight she felt like she couldn't get enough oxygen. "Yeah, okay."

He kissed her forehead, and then turned to Chase, who was walking back toward them, after dropping J.J. off with his wife. "Chase, we'll be back in a couple hours. I've got my phone. Let me know if Emily has any issues, okay?"

"Sure thing." Chase gave Jaimi another curious glance, then smiled at her, a kind, beautiful smile that made her heart tighten. "Dane's a great guy," he said to her. "He's like my brother. Be good to him."

His words weren't a warning. They were more like an offering of a gift, and they made her throat tighten yet again. Silently, she nodded, unable to come up with words.

"See? I told you I was a great guy." Dane winked at Chase. "I keep trying to tell her, but she's tough to convince. Thanks for the backup."

"No problem." One of the women behind him called his name, and Chase grinned at Jaimi. "Mira thinks I'm a great guy, and I need to keep up the illusion. It was great to meet you. Emily will have a fantastic time. Don't worry about her. Just go have fun." He turned away before she could answer, striding across the snow toward a woman sitting on a beach chair.

For a long moment, Jaimi just stood there, unable to tear herself away.

"You want to go with them?" Dane asked.

Longing coursed through her, desperate, almost painful longing. She wanted to say yes. God, she wanted to say yes... but at the same time, she wanted to run away, fast, and never look back. She took a deep breath. "No."

"You sure?"

She looked at him, wanting to change the subject. "I'm going to go back to Boston tomorrow, so you have two hours to grill me to find out what you want to know."

His brows shot up. "Tomorrow? I thought you were here all week."

"I changed my mind."

"When?"

"About a millisecond ago."

He laughed, a deep rumble that seemed to wrap around

her. He didn't look concerned by her deadline announcement. Instead, he turned her toward him and slid his arms around her waist, in a move that was decidedly intimate and not at all in alignment with a sheriff interrogating her. And, she wasn't going to lie, she absolutely loved how it felt to be in his arms. He eyed her, amusement twinkling in his brown eyes. "Well, if I have only a couple hours, I better get on it. I can't afford to waste a minute."

She swallowed, all her emotions completely in an uproar, between seeing all the Stocktons, and Dane manhandling her waist so deliciously. "No, definitely not. What do you want to know?"

"Mmm... I'm sort of curious whether your lips are cold. It's pretty chilly out."

She swallowed again. "My lips?"

"Yeah. Are they cold?"

"I don't know. I hadn't really thought about it—"

"You don't know? I'll check. Fact-finding is an addiction of mine. It's another one of those cop things." He cocked his brow, and leaned in until his lips were only an inch from hers. "You mind?"

Oh, God. There was no Emily around to stop them this time. "I don't date," she whispered, her voice slightly breathless. "I already told you."

"And I told you that was okay. I'm an expert dater." He grinned. "You know, asking if your lips were cold was actually a ploy to get you to let me kiss you. I'm not really on some mission to investigate skin temperature, you know. See? That's what happens when you're courted by a guy who's an expert on dating. You get kissed without even having to acknowledge it, and so you avoid all the emotional pitfalls. I'm like a boy scout, I'm so damned helpful."

She started laughing. "You're insane."

"And kissable, right? Because you're super kissable, and I

know I'm super kissable, so that means if you put us together, we might spontaneously explode from kissability, and that is definitely the way I want to go." He tightened his grip around her waist. "So, I'll ask again." He gave her a completely serious look that made her start laughing again. "Jaimi Hamilton, would you please allow me to conduct research on skin temperatures in Rogue Valley, Wyoming three days before Christmas? Purely scientific, with absolutely nothing to do with how damn much I've been wanting to kiss you ever since you threw yourself onto my lap when the tractor drove harmlessly past."

She burst out laughing. "I threw myself onto your lap?"

"Yes." He slid one hand behind the back of her neck, his fingers nestling in the nape of her neck. "It was how I knew you were interested in me. My expertise in dating has taught me that unless a woman throws herself into my lap in front of a speeding tractor, she is not the least bit attracted to me. If she does, however, it means she's green-lighting me to unleash my devastatingly charming personality onto her." He grinned. "So let's stop messing around, let's just make out for a couple seconds, before we head out and grab some dinner. Sound good?"

"I'm not the type of girl to make out," she said firmly. At his comically crestfallen expression, she started laughing, completely unable to resist how happy he made her feel. "But as a teacher, I'm a big fan of doing research and fact-finding before drawing conclusions."

Dane's face brightened. "Hot damn. That's the best news I've heard in at least thirty seconds. I am all in for research." He got a decidedly nefarious expression on his face as he locked his arm tighter around her waist, and buried his other hand deeper in her hair at the nape of her neck. "I love research."

Then he pulled her against him, angled his head, and

kissed her.

CHAPTER 12

$\mathcal{T}$he moment Dane's lips touched hers, Jaimi knew she was lost.

Lost in him. Lost in the kiss. Lost in how he made her feel. Lost in the most delicious way possible. The kind of lost where you actually feel like you finally have more answers than you've ever had before, the kind of lost where you drop all the barriers that have trapped you for so long, and you just breathe in the beauty of the moment that you're in. Where you stop hanging onto everything and stop trying to control everything.

The kind of lost she hadn't known existed until this very moment.

It had been one thing when he'd kissed her on the fence post. That had been unexpected, magical, and super fun and flirty. He had surprised her, and made her feel beautiful and appealing.

This one was different. This one felt like it was so much more. It wasn't simply that the kiss was deeper, that this kiss was slower and more sensual, as if he were carefully stoking the fires buried deep within her.

It was different because she wasn't afraid of him anymore. When he'd kissed her before, she'd still been anxiously waiting for him to start prying away at her secrets. She'd been afraid that he would find out who she was, how scared she was, and hate her for it.

All that was gone now, and all that was left was a man who knew her truth, the one she was most afraid of revealing, and he'd proven himself to be strong, supportive, and understanding. The way he'd carried Emily and tucked Jaimi against his side as they had approached the Stocktons, somehow sensing how nervous they both were, had been amazing. He'd offered them his strength, and he'd done it in a way that had made both of them feel like they could take on that which scared them the most.

And, most importantly, he'd honored her request to keep her secret private. A secret which affected those who had been his family his whole life. For some reason, he had chosen her side, and that felt so beautiful she could barely even understand how it made her feel.

He slid his hand under her jacket, spreading his fingers on the bare skin of her lower back as he continued to kiss her. A low groan escaped Jaimi's lips as she leaned into him, gripping the front of his jacket, as if she were afraid that he would stop. It felt so good to feel the heat and hardness of his body pressed against hers. She was stunned by how incredible it felt to have his arm locked around her waist, to feel the warmth of his hand against the back of her neck. She felt safe, encircled by his strength.

He deepened the kiss still more, a kiss that was no longer about anything except them. She wanted to get closer to him. She wanted to kiss him back more deeply. She wanted to pour her soul into the kiss, and offer it into his capable hands for safekeeping.

She'd been kissed before, more than once, more than

twice, but never had a kiss made her feel so beautiful, so safe, and so loved, as Dane's kiss was doing right then.

This time she wasn't holding any secrets anymore. This time she wasn't afraid of what he was going to find out. This time he knew he was kissing a woman who was scared, vulnerable, alone, and secretly related to his best friends. This time he knew he was kissing a woman that he knew wasn't always strong, sassy, and funny.

And the fact that he knew all that about her, and was kissing her anyway, made it so much more beautiful. She felt the kiss all the way deep inside her, in her belly, in her breath, and in her heart.

There was something about Dane that lifted her spirits in a way she hadn't thought was possible. She loved the sensation of his lips on her, the way he so effortlessly turned the kiss into something deeper, something sensual, something with a little bit of decadence.

There was a sudden roar from the crowd, screams and applause erupting around them. Jaimi pulled back quickly, and looked around, half expecting everyone to be looking at her and catcalling her.

No one cared what she and Dane had been doing.

Everyone was looking past her toward the stage, so she turned around just as Travis Turner walked out onto the stage, only a few yards away from them. He pointed at the Stocktons and blew them kisses, before grabbing the mic and issuing a booming Christmas welcome to the town of Rogue Valley.

It was the Travis Turner she'd seen in so many videos online, the Travis Turner who filled up a large portion of her playlist, the Travis Turner that she and Emily had cranked in the car on the way to school so many times.

And it was also her brother. "Holy crap. That's really my brother?"

Dane laughed as he slid his arms around her waist, drawing her back against his chest, and resting his chin on her shoulder. "Yeah," he said. "It's good to have him back around. He took off from Rogue Valley for a long time. It wasn't until he met Lissa that he settled here again."

"Why did he leave?" She leaned back against Dane, resting her head on his shoulder as she watched Travis chatting with the crowd, making them laugh and feel welcome.

Dane didn't answer, and she twisted around to look at him. His face was troubled, his eyes shadowed.

She frowned and twisted around in his arms to face him. She rested her forearms against his chest, and searched his face. "What's wrong?"

His face became even more troubled, and for a moment she thought he wasn't even going to meet her gaze. But after a few seconds, he finally looked at her. "How much do you know about your biological father?"

Her stomach jumped. "Nothing. I didn't even know his name until my mom told me about my brothers a few weeks ago. I assume his last name is Stockton? Is he alive? What's he like?" She hadn't even thought about her father. Her mom had mentioned only her brothers, and given her the list of names. She'd been so consumed with her siblings, and so happy with her mom as her only parent, that she hadn't even wasted any time on thinking about a dad. "What do you know about him?"

Dane sighed and lightly trailed his finger along her jaw. "Why don't we grab some grub and find somewhere to eat? We can talk there."

She stared at him, her heart sinking. "Why aren't you telling me now?"

"Because I don't know how, and I need time to figure it out."

Jaimi suddenly felt cold, very, very cold. "Tell me now."

Dane sighed. "Jaimi—"

She pushed at his chest. "Tell me, Dane. I want to know."

He caught her wrists. "I swear I will tell you, but this is not the place." He gestured to the crowds, to the Stocktons nearby. "Emily will be back out here to watch the show any second. Let's go find a place we can talk."

"But—"

He pressed a kiss to each of her balled fists, his gaze beseeching hers. "Trust me on this one, Jaimi. You need to."

Something about the way he said it made something heavy settle in her stomach, something weighty, and scared. Suddenly, she didn't want to know. She didn't want to know any of it. She'd gone her whole life without knowing, and there was no reason to find out now. "You know, I think I'm good. Why don't I just head back to the hotel—"

Dane cut her off with a kiss that went from bossy to molten within moments. He didn't break the kiss until her arms were around his neck and she was sagging against him, nothing but a melted ball of mush.

He pulled back, smiling as he kissed the tip of her nose. "No more running away, sweetheart. Let's go get food, and hunker down. Okay?"

She took a deep breath, and let it out slowly. He was right. She didn't actually want to run away. It just felt like it was too much to handle, but with Dane's hands locked around her hips, and his body against hers, she felt like maybe she could do it. "Okay."

He grinned, a smile that didn't reach his eyes anymore. "Okay."

Jaimi let him take her hand, and she followed him as he threaded his way through the crowd, who was now singing along with Travis to his trademark song, *Fence Sittin'.* She glanced back over her shoulder at the Stocktons, and saw that another Stockton had joined them, one she hadn't met yet, but he looked very much like Maddox. A twin? Didn't Maddox have a twin brother? Ryder, right? She was pretty sure that was it.

Ryder was watching her, and the look on his face was hard, as if he were ready to do whatever it took to defend his family, if she proved to be a threat. The darkness of his expression made her swallow, and she looked at Dane's face as she followed him.

He, too, had lost the lightness that had made her feel so good. He looked hard, like a man who had been through hell and survived. Then he looked over at her and smiled, transforming his expression back to the one she'd gotten to know.

Except now she knew better. She knew that underneath Dane's light-hearted exterior lay something else. Something darker, something that she might not like, something that she might not be strong enough to handle.

CHAPTER 13

"he tractor that almost killed me?" Jaimi stopped when she realized where Dane was taking them.

He grinned. "It's our special place, sweetheart. I'm extremely romantic, and it feels that it's fitting to celebrate our three hours meet-i-versary in the place we met."

"Meet-i-versary?"

"Yeah. The anniversary of our first meeting. Romantic, right?"

She gave him a skeptical look. "Are we going to have to come here for every three-hour anniversary for the rest of our lives?"

His heart did a little jump at her question. He knew she wasn't serious, but the mere fact her mind had gone to "the rest of our lives," made him damned happy. "Nah. Once we can start talking in years, we can skip the three-hour anniversary celebrations, and just go with once a day. I think that's reasonable. What was it, like six o'clock when we met?"

She started to laugh. "You're a nut case. You realize that, don't you?"

"Yeah, I work at it. I also want to sit here because if we sit any closer, I'm going to be constantly on duty as sheriff. If we're back here, lurking in the shadows like the criminal I always wanted to be, people won't bother us." He tucked his hand under her arms and guided her toward the tractor that was now safely parked on the edge of the festival grounds. The trailer was still filled with hay bales and loose hay, but there was a sign on it that told people to keep off because it was closed.

He walked right past the sign, grinning when Jaimi raised her eyebrows. "More sheriff privileges?"

"No, just payback because I'm not going to give him any parking or driving citations for the rest of his life."

"Why not?"

"Because his reckless driving made us meet." He set their dinner on top of a hay bale, then held out his hand to give Jaimi a hand up.

She just stared at him. "You meant that. I could hear it in your voice. You really are a romantic, aren't you?"

"Yep." He waggled his fingers at her. "Let's go, sweetheart. Travis only plays for a couple hours so we don't have time to waste."

Her smile faded. "What if I don't want to talk? Can we just listen to the concert?"

His heart softened, and he walked over to her, encircling her wrists with his hands. He knew that he needed to tell her the truth, and he couldn't tell her that it would be okay, that it would all work out, because he didn't know how she would react. He wouldn't make promises he couldn't keep, so instead of answering, he just leaned down and kissed her.

She sighed and leaned into the kiss, a kiss that was perfect, beautiful, and tender, the kind of kiss he wished would last forever, and lead to so much more.

But instead of scooping her up in his arms and carrying her off to his bedroom for the kind of kisses he really wanted to do, he forced himself to break the kiss, finishing off with a little peck to the tip of her nose.

She sighed, gazing up at him dreamily. "Can't we just make out for a couple hours instead?"

He grinned. "Let's talk fast, and then make out the rest of the time. Good?"

"Okay. Let's set a timer for two minutes. Deal?"

"Deal." But even as he agreed, he had a bad feeling that she might not be in the mood for kissing once he told her the truth about the family she came from.

She gave him a tentative smile that made his heart turn over, then she took his hand and climbed up onto the trailer. He followed swiftly with the three heavy blankets he'd grabbed from his truck.

Within a couple minutes, they were side by side, nestled under the blankets, with their food on their laps, with a thousand unspoken things hanging between them. As they sat there, the silence building between them, he found himself searching for the right words, the words that would tell her about the father she never knew, about the childhood her brothers had...but the words wouldn't come.

He had no idea how to tell her.

And she didn't ask. She just leaned against him, eating her dinner, and singing under her breath to the music, knowing every word of every song that her brother had written. Her face was beautiful under the moon, and the awe on her face as she watched her brother was enough to make his own heart tighten.

She seemed to sense him watching her, because her gaze flicked to his, and she smiled. "Travis is amazing," she said. "He's so gifted."

"I know." He leaned forward and kissed her gently, brushing the crumbs off her lips with the kiss.

She sighed and smiled at him, completely relaxed,

completely in the moment with him. It was a perfect, romantic moment, under a clear, starry sky, a pile of warm blankets, with a woman who made his heart feel truly alive. It was the kind of night to be remembered forever…and yet he couldn't concentrate on it, not the way he wanted to.

Because he knew he had to rain hell down on her by telling her about the bastard father whose blood ran in her veins.

And the longer they sat there, the harder he knew it would be to tell her.

He had to do it.

He had to be the one to inject a whole shitload of darkness into her life, and he had to do it now, so he could help her deal with it. He'd helped each of her brothers through hell and back over the years, and had hidden from the bastard with each of them, especially Maddox and Ryder. He'd even taken some of the blows so the Stocktons could escape the real wrath. He was a part of that darkness, and he'd worked hard to be a light in that hell. It was his job with the Stocktons, and he knew it was his job with her.

But hell, he didn't want to do this to her. But she deserved to know the truth.

And it was time.

CHAPTER 14

*W*ith a sigh of resolution, Dane set his plate on a nearby hay bale, then he gestured to hers. "Can I take that for a sec?"

She nodded silently, her eyes huge as she stared at him.

He managed a grim smile, then took her plate and set it beside his. Then he faced her, and took her hands in his. Her fingers were cold, and he cupped them tightly, trying to warm them as he searched her face. "Jaimi."

Jaimi caught her breath at the expression on Dane's face. He was going to tell her something bad. Something terrible. She didn't want to know it. She knew she didn't. But at the same time, she knew she couldn't run away. She had to see this entire thing through, and see where she ended up. So she focused on the feel of his hands wrapped around hers. "What?"

He took a deep breath. "Jaimi, your dad—"

No. She suddenly leaned forward and kissed him, cutting him off. Her move was pure instinct, pure avoidance, but the moment her lips touched his, she forgot about everything but *him*.

He sighed and kissed her back immediately, his hands sliding to the back of her neck and into her hair as she leaned into him. His response was so without hesitation and so complete that her heart melted just a little bit. This amazing man was as called to her as she was to him.

She hadn't felt this caught up in a man in ages, maybe ever. She'd held herself alone for so long, and she was proud of how independent she was. She'd learned how to be a badass single mom from her own mother, and she'd never wanted a man to interfere in her life. She didn't need a man. She'd never really yearned for a man.

But there had always been something inside her, something so deep that she could barely even fathom it, that had burned for a deep connection. She yearned for that soul-deep bond with another human, a bond that was different from a mother-daughter connection. A bond as a woman, as a human being, as an equal, and as something more, something beautiful and romantic. Something like what she felt with Dane.

She knew she was going back to Boston. She knew there was no future with Dane. But in this moment, she wanted to feel alive, in the way she'd felt only in Dane's arms.

He groaned softly and leaned into the kiss, easing her back until they were both lying down, their legs and bodies tangled around each other, deep beneath the heavy blankets. The air was cold on her face, but her body was hot and fiery against his.

"Damn, Jaimi." Dane tossed his cowboy hat aside, and then bent his head, nibbling on her neck as his weight settled on her. His pelvis was pressed against hers, hard and ready, making desire pulse through her entire body. He lowered himself on top of her, easing his weight down in a delicious, tantalizing move that made her entire body hum with joy.

She wrapped her arms around his neck, holding him

close as he angled his head, deepening the kiss, pouring sensuality and seduction into her. With a throaty sigh that seemed to come from somewhere deep inside her, she hooked her feet over his calves, basking in the pure strength of his body. He was pure muscle, untamed and unbound, and yet, at the same time, his kisses were so tender, so nurturing, so protective, that she knew her heart and her body would be safe with him forever, no matter what.

He shifted his weight to the side, and slid his hand beneath her jacket, his hand palming her belly. Somehow, his hand was warm, and her entire body seemed to melt at the feel of his skin against hers. He moved his hand upward, grazing her ribs as he deepened the kiss, stoking fires in her that seemed to build with each touch, each kiss, each time he whispered her name.

Within moments, the kiss seemed to ignite, and suddenly, neither of them could get enough. The kiss became deep and more sensual, more powerful, drawing both of them more and more tightly into its web of desire. His body pressed more heavily into her, and suddenly, his hand was beneath her bra, cupping her breast as if it were this great treasure he would protect forever.

Tears suddenly filled her eyes, overwhelming her. Dane broke the kiss almost instantly, pulling back just enough to see her face. "Hey, sweetheart, what's wrong?"

She gazed up at him, at the way he was leaning over her, concern etched on his handsome features. Somehow, he'd known instantly the moment her emotions had over-whelmed her. He hadn't been able to see her face. He hadn't heard her voice break. There had been no way for him to know, and yet he had, and his worry for her had broken through his sexual haze instantly.

Tears threatened again, and she laid her hand against his cheek. "I've never felt as treasured as you make me feel," she whispered. "It's so beautiful. Thank you for being so kind to me."

His expression softened, and he turned his head to press a kiss against her palm. "You deserve only kindness," he said gently. "How is it possible that no one has ever treated you like this before? What about Emily's dad?"

She watched him as he scattered tiny kisses along the underside of her wrist. "Emily's dad was just a guy who I thought I loved for a very short time. He left long before Emily was born, and that was okay with me. He gave me the gift of my daughter, and I'll always be so incredibly grateful for that."

Dane paused, his dark eyes searching her. "Did he know you were pregnant when he left?"

Jaimi nodded. "It was fine that he left. Raising Emily by myself made me stronger, because it gave me the freedom to be who I wanted to be."

Dane frowned. "Sweetheart, it's not fine. You deserve someone who loves you and respects you, who will help you with everything that you want your life to be, both as a mother, and as a woman."

Jaimi's throat tightened. "It's impossible to be in a relationship and still be true to yourself."

"Oh, baby, that's not true." He rolled onto his side, propping himself up on his elbow. His gaze was intense and fierce, somehow wrapping her up in a feeling of warmth. "I'm not going to lie, there are a ton of self-absorbed assholes in this world who would rather drag you down than boost you up, but it doesn't have to be this way. In the right relationship, you're a thousand times stronger, and your partner helps you find that true self that you want to be."

She stared up at him, shocked by his words. "That sounds..." She didn't even know.

"Beautiful? Right? The way life should be?" He smiled, stroking her hair back from her face. "Sweetheart, the reason I'm still single even though I believe the most important thing I will do in my life is be a husband and dad is because I know that if the relationship isn't the right one, it'll break you. I've been holding out for the real thing, the one where my soul knows that it has found the one that it was meant to find."

Her heart caught. "That's so beautiful."

He smiled. "I thought so for a long time, until I finally started to give up hope that I was going to find it. I'd rather stay single than be with the wrong person, and I'd finally started to believe it wasn't going to happen, not for me, not in this lifetime."

"And then?"

"And then some woman threw herself in my lap."

God, he meant *her*. He meant those beautiful words for *her*. "You don't even know me," she whispered.

"Getting to know someone takes more than a lifetime," he said. "But there's a point at which you know, with every bit of your heart, that this is the person you want to build your life with, the one whose hand you want to hold through every adventure that life delivers."

As she stared at him, the most agonizingly desperate yearning coursed through her, a need so strong that it almost made her want to cry. "I could never trust this," she whispered. "I could never turn myself over to you, to a forever, to what I'm feeling right now—"

"It's okay." He kissed her gently. "Trust takes time. I'm not going anywhere."

"But I am. I'm going back to Boston—"

"Now?"

She shook her head. "No, but—"

"Then we have now." He bent his head and kissed her

again, a kiss so tender that there was no way for her to stop the tears this time.

Dane again stopped kissing her, but this time, he traced his thumbs over her cheeks, wiping away the tears. He then pressed tender, little kisses over her cheeks, as if he himself could provide enough sunshine to dry them, and she almost felt like he could.

She closed her eyes and breathed in the sensation of his lips brushing over her cheeks, of his arm resting heavily across her stomach, of his hand gripping her hip, of his legs stretched out alongside hers. "This feels so perfect," she whispered. "How does this feel so perfect?"

"Because it's the start of what we've both been looking for our whole lives."

"I haven't been looking for this," she protested. "I wasn't looking for Wyoming, I wasn't looking for brothers, and I wasn't looking to fall in love. I just wanted to fulfill my promise to my mom."

He smiled, the most beautiful smile she'd ever seen. "Maybe your mind wasn't looking for this, but what about your heart?" He rested his hand over her heart. "Listen to the whispers deep inside," he said. "What are they saying?"

Dane. "Your name," she admitted.

He grinned. "Thank God for that. If you'd said they were saying Malcom or something like that, I was going to wish I'd taken a different tactic."

She burst out laughing, relieved by his sense of humor. "Yeah, that would have been super awkward."

"I know, right?" He grinned and rolled on top of her again, pinning her down. "I find myself completely resenting the thousands of people who have come to support my tiny town tonight. If they weren't here, I could ravish you right here on this trailer. You'd be amazed at the ideas in my head right now."

She grinned. "You couldn't ravish me anyway. I never have sex on the first date."

"Damn. I don't like to wait. We should break up now."

"We can't break up. We aren't a couple."

He feigned a horrified look. "We aren't? I never kiss a woman that I'm not coupled with. We need to change that fast. Will you be my hot girlfriend?"

She laughed. "No. I don't date."

"Well, hell." He eyed her speculatively. "How are we going to fix this, then?"

"Not kiss?"

"Maybe. Let's see." He bent his head and kissed her, a kiss that was so devastatingly hot that she was pretty much on fire by the time he stopped. He cocked his head. "What do you think? Should we stop doing that?"

"I kind of like being set on fire in the middle of winter, so maybe not."

"Yeah, I agree. So, maybe meet in the middle? I agree to kiss a woman that I'm only casually dating, as opposed to seriously coupled with, and you agree that we are casually dating. How does that sound?"

Her amusement faded, replaced by a tightness in her chest. "You mean that, don't you?"

"Of course, I do."

"How can we date? I live in Boston."

"Are you there now?"

"No, but—"

He held up his hand. "Why don't you try just going with it? Just say yes, and see what happens. I'm a great guy. You'd love to casually date me, I'm sure."

She searched his face, surprised by how badly she wanted to say yes. But how could she? She didn't know how to date. She didn't know how to trust a man. She didn't know how to partner with anyone. She didn't—

Her protests died as she looked at Dane, at his handsome face, at the kindness in his eyes. Her heart wanted to say yes. It was *screaming* at her to say yes.

Dane searched her face. "Just say yes, Jaimi. Take a chance."

She swallowed, her heart pounding. "I'm afraid," she whispered.

"I know, baby." He smiled. "I'm really good at keeping people safe." He pressed a kiss to her palm. "Give me a chance. Just one. I won't blow it."

Silently, unable to even say it aloud, she nodded.

His face lit up. "That's a yes?"

This time, she found her voice. "Yes, I'll casually date you for the next few days while I'm in town."

"That is the best damn news I've had in at least a minute." He caught her face and kissed her, long, hard, deep, until she was melting in his arms. "Okay, I lied."

She opened her eyes. "About what?"

"That's the best damn news I've had in way longer than a minute."

She grinned and draped her arms around his neck. "Like how long? Lifetime?"

"Yeah, maybe." He cocked his head. "Just might be that long. You?"

"At least five seconds for me."

He nodded. "I've always wanted to be a five-second guy. I consider this a moment of victory." He grinned and kissed her, a kiss that quickly resulted in her being beneath him, completely enraptured by his kisses.

CHAPTER 15

*I*t was almost an hour before Dane had the willpower to stop kissing her. They were snuggled under the blankets, his arms around Jaimi, her head resting on his shoulder, as they listened to Travis sing. Thanks to the presence of a few thousand fans, they were both still fully clothed, which had somehow made everything even more intimate. All they could do was kiss, and it had been a long damned time since he'd spent an hour kissing a woman.

He knew the order of songs Travis had planned for the evening, and he knew they were running out of time. "Sweetheart?"

"Hmm?"

"We need to talk."

She stiffened against him, a movement so slight that it was almost imperceptible. "You want to know why I don't know my brothers?"

"Well, yeah, that and I need to tell you about your dad. Which do you want to do first?"

She was quiet for a moment. "I'll talk," she said quietly. "I think it would feel good."

Something settled inside him at the realization that she trusted him. "I've got you."

"I know." She began to play with the buttons on his shirt. "I grew up in Boston with my mom. She was a teacher, too. It was just the two of us. She never dated, and she always told me that my dad had died before I was born. She was an amazing mom, and I never missed having a dad."

Guilt tore at Dane's gut, guilt for what he was going to have to tell her. "You had a good childhood?"

"A wonderful one. I was so happy." She sighed. "When Emily was born, and it became the three of us, we were a powerful force. I felt strong and invincible, like I didn't need anyone."

He could feel the "but" coming. "What happened?"

"A few months ago, my mom went on a backpacking trip on the Amazon river—"

"The Amazon river? Seriously?" Well, damn. No wonder Jaimi was so independent.

"Yeah, she was an adventurer. Nothing ever stopped her, except on this trip, she caught some tropical infection when she went swimming—"

"Swimming in the Amazon? With crocodiles? And snakes?"

"Yeah." The affection in Jaimi's voice was evident. "She was a lot bolder than I am. But she got bitten by something, and it got infected. She decided not to cut her trip short, and it got worse. I tried to get her to come home, but she refused."

Dane tightened his arms around her. "What happened?"

"She video-called me from some village a couple weeks ago." Jaimi's voice was heavy. "She looked terrible, and admitted that she was dying. Apparently, whatever had bitten her was extremely poisonous. She said she couldn't die without telling me about my brothers. She said she'd been on a cross-country backpacking trip when she was in her twenties, and had a brief fling as she was passing through Rogue Valley. Apparently, a few years ago, she decided to see if he was still around, and she discovered I had all these brothers. She'd left Chase's picture in her desk, and told me where to find it. She made me give her a deathbed promise that I'd track them down." Jaimi could still feel that shock when her mom had made that last call. "I promised, of course, but I told her she wasn't allowed to die in the freaking Amazon."

"And?"

"She ignored me, and died that night. One of the others in her group called me the next day and said she'd died. She'd already made arrangements to be cremated by the village and released into the forest to nourish the earth, so that was it. She'd always said she wanted to be cremated and released into the Charles River, which was, of course, highly illegal, but apparently, the Amazon had become her new resting place." That still annoyed her just a little bit. She knew her mom was independent, but it would have been a little thoughtful to let her only child have the closure of being able to do the ceremonial end-of-life thing.

Dane swore. "She sounds pretty damn bold. I wish I could have met her."

"Yeah, she was amazing. Emily is just like her, but I'm nowhere near the woman she was." Jaimi rested her head on Dane's shoulder, breathing in the feel of his arms around her. "She told me I wasn't allowed to be sad."

Dane pressed a kiss to her head, a kiss so tender that her throat tightened. "It's okay to grieve, sweetheart."

"She'll come back from the grave and shoot me if I waste my life being sad," Jaimi said. "And I think she's right. She lived an amazing life all the way to the end, and if I could live with a fraction of that spirit, I'd be thrilled. I'm working on it, but I spend half my time being afraid." She sighed. "I know I sound all tough, but I'm not, at least compared to her."

Dane sighed, gently stroking her hair. "It's okay to find your own path. You don't have to be like your parents. Sometimes, it's better not to be."

His words hung like a weight in the air, and she knew he was referring to her father. With a deep breath, she sat up and faced him, trying to channel her mother, and find courage she wasn't sure she had. "Tell me, Dane. Tell me about him."

Dane sat up, facing her, his face serious. "He doesn't matter," he said gently. "You have become this amazing and powerful woman, with an incredible role model in your mom. It doesn't matter who your father was—"

"*Was*? So, he's dead?" A flash of sadness engulfed her, sadness for the man she hadn't bothered to think about her whole life. "Before I was born? Like my mom said?"

"He died about ten years ago."

"Ten?" She blinked, her throat suddenly tight. "So, I could have known him? I could have met him?"

Dane swore under his breath and took her hands. "Jaimi —" He paused, and she looked at him, searching his face.

"What, Dane? *What?*"

"He wasn't a good guy."

She waited for more, but Dane didn't say anything else. "Tell me. What does that mean?"

Hell. Dane had no idea how to tell her. She was so beautiful, her soul was so pure, and she was so strong. But at the same time, she was so vulnerable. "Jaimi—"

"Dammit, Dane. Stop messing with me. Just tell me!" She pulled back, her hands balled into fists.

Dane ground his jaw, knowing that she deserved to know, and that she deserved to know from him, not from some stranger. "Your dad was an abusive alcoholic," he said finally.

She blinked. "What? You mean, like to his sons?"

"Yeah, to his sons. To their friends. To their girlfriends. To their mothers. He was a bad guy."

She stared at him, her face so crestfallen that he could barely make himself continue. "Mothers? They have different ones?"

"Yeah. Your nine brothers have seven different mothers. Some of them he married, others he didn't. Most of the women he brought into the home were not good people. The only way your brothers survived was by sticking together."

She stared at him, her face shocked. "How bad was it?" Her voice was a raw whisper.

Fuck. He had to tell her. He knew he did. But he didn't want to. He could go into gruesome detail with example after example, but he didn't want to. There was one incident that would sum it all up, and spare her the details. "Chase killed him to save Travis's life when Travis was sixteen," he said softly.

"What?" She began to scramble backwards, as if she could get away from what he'd told her. "Chase *murdered* my father?"

"No!" Dane lunged to his feet, catching her wrist as she stood up. "Chase *saved* Travis' life, because he is a born protector. Your brothers are the most heroic and honorable men I know. They protected and defended each other as best they could."

"So, my father tried to murder his own son, and my brother killed him in return? My family is all a bunch of *murderers*?" Her face became stricken. "The man who's watching my daughter is a *killer*? Dear God, Dane, what have you done?" Her voice was panicked now, pitched with fear as she lunged for the edge of the trailer.

Dane swore and leapt to the ground, catching her as she landed. "Jaimi—"

"No!" She shoved at his hands. "I need to go get Emily—"

"Listen to me!" He clasped her shoulders. "Every single one of your brothers is a good man. They aren't like your father."

"Not like him? They killed him! *Killed*!" She tore herself free and sprinted past him, racing in a desperate sprint toward the Stocktons.

Shit. He'd completely fucked it up. Swearing, he broke into a sprint, ducking around people as he rushed to catch up to Jaimi before she got to the Stocktons.

~

He was too late.

The concert had ended just as Jaimi had raced away from him, and it took Dane too damn long to get through the multitude of festival attendees wanting to talk to their sheriff. People were packing up their belongings, chatting happily as they milled about, making it almost impossible for Dane to navigate quickly.

By the time he got to the Stocktons, Jaimi was nowhere to be seen, and the Stocktons were all standing around, looking startled.

Fuck. What had she said?

Swearing under his breath, Dane walked up, trying to appear casual. "Did Jaimi come by?"

Everyone looked at him, but Chase was the one who answered. "Yeah, she came by, like a bat out of hell. She retrieved her daughter and took off so fast that she almost trampled Zane."

Dane swore. "What did she say?"

"Not much," Zane said. "She grabbed her daughter, muttered something about having to leave, and then bolted."

Relieved that she hadn't called Chase a murderer, Dane let out his breath. "Which way did she go?"

Zane pointed toward the parking lot.

Shit. She was leaving. "I gotta go." He whirled around to go after her, when Chase's voice stopped him cold.

"Why didn't you tell us?"

Slowly, Dane turned around to face Chase. Every single Stockton, and their wives, were watching him. "Tell you what?" he asked evasively.

"You think we're blind?" Ryder said. "What the hell do you think is wrong with us?"

Hell. "I don't know what you mean."

"Stockton eyes," Maddox said evenly. "That little girl has Stockton eyes, and we all know damn well that you saw it, too."

Fuck.

"And her mom has the Stockton cheekbones," Chase added. "You had to have seen it, and you delivered them right to us. What the hell is going on, Dane?"

Dane looked around at the men he considered his family, who had been his only bright light when he was a kid going through a hell not that different from theirs. "I promised her I wouldn't tell."

"Fuck that," Zane said. "You're choosing her over us? What the hell is wrong with you?"

"He loves her," Chase said quietly. "Look at the expression on his face."

Dane quickly tried to assume a neutral expression. "I need to go after her. She's upset, and she might be leaving town—"

"Then you better talk fast, because your ass isn't going anywhere until you spill." Ryder folded his arms over his chest. "What the hell, Dane?"

He looked at Ryder and Maddox, the twins, standing side by side, and guilt shot through him. He'd been tight with all the Stocktons, but he was the same age as the twins, and they'd spent the most time together. They were his brothers. His family. His everything. Swearing, he finally sighed. "If I tell you, do you all swear not to do anything? To let me handle it?"

The brothers and their wives all looked at each other, then Chase spoke for them. "If we agree with how you want to handle it, yeah. If not, no."

That wasn't good enough. He knew what family meant to them, and he knew that if they went after Jaimi now, they would all lose her forever. She was running scared, and he needed to get to her first. He knew he could help her, but he needed to find her first, before the Stocktons descended. "I need a promise. You all give me forty-eight hours before you do anything. And I mean *anything.* If you won't swear to give me that time to work with Jaimi, I'm telling you nothing. And since I'm the one with the gun and the badge, you all know damn well you can't stop me if I turn around and walk away right now."

Was it wrong that he played the sheriff card for his own personal use? Probably. But right now, he didn't care.

Chase swore and looked around. One by one, each of the brothers nodded. Dane then looked at Mira and Taylor, waiting until Mira finally threw up her hands. "Fine, we promise, too."

Taylor rolled her eyes, but she nodded. "Fine."

Lissa, Hannah, and Erin all nodded as well. "We promise."

"Okay, then." Dane gritted his teeth, knowing that all hell was going to break loose when he told them. If he had actually been a member of the family, they might even disown him when they found out he'd kept it a secret that they had family. Glancing quickly at his watch, he nodded. "Two minutes, and then I'm going after her."

Zane gestured to a chair. "Two minutes."

Dane ignored the chair. Instead, he looked around at his brothers. He took a deep breath, and then dropped the bomb that he knew would shock the tight-knit siblings to their core. "You guys have a sister."

CHAPTER 16

*S*ilence.

After Dane's announcement, there was absolute, stone-cold silence.

For about one second, and then all hell broke loose. They all started talking so fast that it was impossible to discern the different questions, or answer any of them. So he didn't try. He just held up his hand and waited until everyone finally stopped talking. "Here's what I know," he said. "Her mom came through town about twenty-five years ago and had a fling with your dad. She then left town and raised Jaimi by herself in Boston. Jaimi didn't know about you guys until two weeks ago, until her mom made her promise to track you all down as her deathbed wish—"

"Her mother's dead?" Steen asked, going straight to worrying about her well-being, as Dane knew they would. "Is Jaimi married? What about Emily's dad?"

"It's just the two of them now."

"We need to go after her," Zane said. "No Stockton stands alone—"

"Why'd she run?" Chase asked, looking at Dane, not

moving from his spot. "Why did she look like she'd seen the devil himself when she came back here?"

Chase's question made everyone else fall silent.

Dane took a deep breath. "When she arrived, she wasn't sure whether she wanted to reveal who she was. Emily wanted to tell you guys, but Jaimi wasn't ready."

Zane whistled softly. "Emily knew the whole time? Damn, that kid is good. She never gave away anything."

Chase looked at him. "When Jaimi came back just now, she was different. What happened?"

Dane sighed. "I told her about her biological father. I told her how he died."

Chase let out a low groan, and a couple of the other brothers did the same. "And now she's on the run," Chase said. "Trying to get the hell away from the same childhood that haunts all of us."

"She thinks we're still monsters," Maddox said quietly, a man who knew that fear all too well, because he'd spent his life believing he was the same monster as his father. Only Hannah's love and her daughter's trust had convinced Maddox that he was a good man.

"Yeah. She kinda freaked." Kinda was an understatement.

Zane looked at Dane. "We aren't going to let her go, you know. She's family."

"I know, but she's scared." Dane held up his hands as everyone started talking again. "Let me go talk to her, and get her to at least stay in town. I'll let you guys know how she is."

"I want to meet her officially," Chase said. "I want to meet her as her brother."

"I know, but right now, you'll spook her." He looked directly at Mira, knowing that she was the core behind the brother. "Shut him down, Mira. This is important. I need to handle this."

Mira nodded and walked over to Chase, slipping her hand into his. "Trust Dane," she said gently. "Give him time."

Chase swore and looked at his brothers. They all had varying expressions of hope, awe, and tension on their faces. "Tomorrow. We'll give you until tomorrow."

"You said forty-eight hours."

Chase looked at him. "She's our *sister*, Dane—"

"Which means you'll do what's right for her, and right now, backing off is what's right. Forty-eight hours." Dane looked at Chase. "In her eyes, you're a murderer, Chase. If you walk up to her right now, she's going to run like hell."

Pain flashed across Chase's face, but Dane couldn't afford to feel regret. The situation was dicey, and he knew he was the glue holding the pieces together.

Ryder finally stepped forward. "I trust Dane," he said. "Go, bro. Fix this."

Dane flashed a grin at the man he'd been closest to as kids. "Thanks." When Ryder nodded at him, Dane knew that Ryder would do whatever it took to keep Chase and the others at bay until Dane could connect with her.

He didn't waste any more time. He just turned and sprinted toward the parking lot, hoping that he could somehow find her among the masses of cars beginning to exit. But even as he ran, he knew the odds were low, so he started formulating alternate plans.

There was no way in hell he was going to fail at this. There was too much at stake, for his brothers, for Jaimi, for Emily, and for his own damn heart.

～

"WHAT DO YOU MEAN, you gave away our room?" Jaimi's hands were still shaking, and she could barely think straight. All she wanted to do was get into her room, lock the door, and hunker down until morning came, and she could get out of town.

The flustered front desk attendant, whose nametag identified her as Peggy, held up her hands helplessly. "I'm so sorry. I wasn't on duty earlier, but check-in is by seven o'clock. We had so many people on the waitlist for the festival that we had to give it away when you didn't check in."

"You didn't have to give it away. You had my credit card —" Jaimi cut herself off, trying to keep herself calm. She knew it wasn't the fault of the woman standing in front of her, but she was so desperate she wanted to cry. "Please, we'll take anything. I have my six-year-old daughter with me. I can't sleep in the car with her!"

"I'm so sorry, but we're at capacity. There are no rooms."

Jaimi took a deep breath, trying to keep the panic at bay. *Her biological father had tried to kill his own son. Her brother had murdered him.* Dear God. She needed to get away, sit down, breathe, think. "Okay, so then, can you at least give me the names of any other hotels in the area?"

Peggy shook her head. "They will all be in the same situation as we are in. Every hotel is overbooked and at capacity due to the festival. People come from hundreds of miles away to attend this."

"So, please, tell me what I can do." She'd already called the airport to try to get a flight that night, but there was nothing until the following afternoon. She had no interest in driving until four in the morning, and then sleeping in an airport. If she was her mom, yeah, she'd probably think it was an adventure. But she wasn't her mom, and she had a child to keep safe. Emily tugged on her hand, but she shook her head. "Just a second, baby."

"Stay with a friend?" Peggy suggested.

"I don't know anyone here. I don't have any friends!"

Emily tugged on her hand again. "Mom!"

She finally looked down, barely able to contain her impatience. "What?"

"Dane's our friend. He'd let us stay with him."

Oh, God. Like she needed that. "I'm sure he would, baby, but I don't have his number. I have no idea how to reach him." Not that she would ever try. She needed to get away from the Stocktons and all connections to them. She turned toward Peggy again. "Are there any B&B's in the area? A—"

"Mom!" Emily poked her in the hip. "You don't need to know his phone number."

Something about Emily's tone caught Jaimi's attention, and she looked down at her daughter again, foreboding welling up inside her. "Why don't I need his phone number?"

Emily pointed toward the lobby. "Because he's standing right there watching us." She waved, and grinned. "Hi, Dane!"

Jaimi closed her eyes as she heard Dane's voice. "Hey, Em."

"Oh…" Peggy's face lit up. "You know Dane? He's *awesome.*" She leaned forward, whispering all too loudly. "He's so handsome, isn't he? Every woman in town has tried to snag him, but no one can get him."

Heat burned Jaimi's cheeks. "Thank you for that info—"

"Hey, Jaimi." He was right behind her. She knew that because of the look of adoration on Peggy's face, her daughter's delighted squeal, and the heat that seemed to be pouring through her from him being so close.

Slowly, she turned around. Her breath caught at the sight of him. His cowboy hat was tipped back on his head, his heavy black jacket framed his muscular shoulders perfectly, and his gorgeous brown eyes focused on her as if she were the only thing in the world that mattered to him. "Hey."

"Hi, Dane." Peggy giggled.

He glanced at Peggy long enough to give her a warm smile. "Good evening, Peggy." Then his attention snapped back to Jaimi. "Are you okay?"

She shrugged.

"She needs a place to crash," Peggy said, leaning forward. "We gave away her room earlier, and we're at capacity. Can she stay at your place?"

Jaimi's cheeks heated up. "We're fine—"

"You can stay with me," Dane said immediately.

"Yay! Mom! Did you hear that? We can stay at Dane's!" Emily shrieked with joy and flung her arms around Dane, who picked her up and settled her against his hip. "We were going to have to sleep in the car," she told Dane. "Grandma slept in a lot of cars when she was younger, but Mommy doesn't think that we should do it. She never lets us sleep in cars, and it's really cold here, so I don't want to do it anyway, you know?"

"I agree. Sleeping in cars in the winter in Wyoming isn't a great idea." He looked over at Jaimi. "We need to talk anyway."

"I don't want to talk."

"I know." He held out his hand. "Come on. You can slap some duct tape over my mouth when we get to my house, but don't skip out on a place that has walls and heat just because I'm an ass who delivered crappy news in a bad way."

"You swore!" Emily announced with delight as she locked her hands around his neck. "You said two bad words!"

Dane's cheeks turned red, and he looked so stricken that some of Jaimi's tension faded. Dane was a good man. She knew it in her heart. It wasn't Dane's fault that her father was a bad person, or that Chase had... Oh, God. She couldn't even think about it. "I don't want to talk about it," she said softly. "I can't."

"Okay." His face softened. "How about I just give you a safe place to crash, then?"

Safe. That sounded so good. And Dane made her feel safe.

It was clear Emily felt safe with him too, and that was a precious gift. "Do you live far from here?"

"Ten minutes. Tops." He held out his hand. "Come on, sweetheart. Let's go."

For a long moment, she stared at his outstretched hand, then finally, she set her hand in his. He squeezed gently, and she felt her entire body sigh deeply and relax at the feel of his hand wrapped so securely around hers. He smiled, and pulled her close enough to give her a little kiss on her forehead before guiding them toward the door. "It'll be okay, sweetheart."

She glanced at him, too weary to argue. "I don't think it will be, Dane. I really don't."

Her mother would have shot her from the grave for being so pessimistic, but hey, her mom was an ash cloud in the Amazon right now, so it didn't really matter what her mom would think.

But it did.

And Jaimi knew she was falling short.

CHAPTER 17

*D*ane folded his arms and leaned against the doorframe between the kitchen and his family room. Emily was fast asleep in his guest bedroom, and Jaimi was curled up on the couch, eating leftover chili, since they hadn't gotten around to finishing their dinner when they were on the trailer.

She looked exhausted, stressed, and absolutely beautiful. He loved the curves of her body beneath her jeans and sweatshirt, and the tight curls of her hair were gorgeous. The flames from the fire were casting an orange glow that illuminated her skin in the most riveting way possible, as if the rich, brown tones of her face were somehow lit from within.

Or maybe it wasn't the reflection of the fire that was doing that. Maybe it was just the light radiating from inside her. "You're breathtaking," he said softly.

She looked up at him, her face softening when she saw him. "I've never had anyone look at me the way you do. There's so much tenderness in your eyes. It's...beautiful."

"You bring it out in me." He levered himself off the door-frame and walked toward her. As he neared, he saw her tense, so he sat down in an armchair facing her, instead of next to her on the couch. "We need to talk."

"I don't want to—"

"We're going to talk anyway." He knew this was his only chance. "Family is important—"

"They aren't my family!" Jaimi pushed the bowl away from her, suddenly not hungry anymore. "I'm going back to Boston in the morning—"

"Give me a chance." He moved quickly, kneeling between her knees, and setting his hands on her hips. "Give me five minutes."

She sucked in her breath at the feel of his hands on her hips. "Why does it feel so good when you touch me?"

"Because it's right." He slid his hand up her arms and drew her face down to his. Jaimi sighed as he kissed her, all her resistance fading at the feel of his lips on hers. After a long, melting kiss, he slid up beside her on the couch, pulling her against him.

She didn't resist.

It simply felt too good, and kissing him seemed like a much better option than revisiting the darkness that apparently ran in her veins. Besides, this was her last chance with him, because she knew that when she left town in the morning, she wasn't coming back.

He broke the kiss. "Jaimi—"

"What about your family?" she interrupted, desperate not to lose this moment by bringing up her biological family. "You know all about mine. What about you?"

He smiled. "Are you practicing avoidance?"

"Totally, but also, since we're casually dating, I think I need to know more about you. How can I casually date someone I don't know every detail about?"

His smile widened. "Definitely practicing avoidance," he said.

"Kiss me, Dane."

"Avoidance works for me." He slid his fingers into her hair and kissed her again, deep, hard, and beautiful.

It took about ten minutes of the most delicious and sensual kissing she'd ever experienced, for Jaimi to admit to herself what she wanted, what she *truly* wanted. "Take me to bed, Dane," she whispered against his mouth.

He went still, his body tensing. "What?"

She sat up. "You aren't seriously going to make me say that twice, are you? I haven't been with anyone since Emily's birth father. I'm a little rusty, and if you make me think about it—"

"I want you to think about it." He sat up, his hand rubbing circles on her lower back. "I already told you that I'm in this for the long haul, Jaimi. I know you don't see a way for this to go anywhere, but that doesn't matter. I believe it will, and I'm not going to screw it up by making a choice that you're not actually ready for."

"Me? What about you?"

"I'm ready for it." He searched her face. "Baby, I'm ready for the whole nine yards, but you're not. You're running scared right now, and I'm going to fiercely protect what we have."

She stared at him. "I don't understand how you can talk like that. How are you so sure? Why do you want me, and this, so much?"

He smiled. "Because I know what it's like."

Her heart suddenly seemed to freeze. "You've already been in love like this?"

"No, not me. My parents." He traced his fingers along her jaw in a move so sensual and beautiful that she got chills. "My parents adored each other. My mom was amazing, and my dad loved the hell out of her. They met when they were in high school. My mom was in a wheelchair, and—"

She stopped him. "A wheelchair? Why?"

"She got sick as a kid, and it left her paralyzed from the waist down. She moved to Rogue Valley when she was fifteen. Kids started bullying her, and my dad stood up for her. He was a star athlete, and he was dating the captain of the women's soccer team at the time. But the minute he met my mom, no one else mattered. He fell in love with her instantly." He smiled, love shining in his eyes. "I loved hearing my dad talk about the first time he saw her. He'd choke up every time, talking about how he knew she was the one for him the moment she smiled at him."

Jaimi's heart turned over. She'd never heard anything like that. Her mom had been an independent warrior, never needing anyone, and she'd taught Jaimi to live that way. The way Dane was talking was...beautiful. There was no other way to describe it. "Tell me more." She tucked her feet under her and turned toward him to listen. "I love their story."

"They married when they were seniors in high school, and she had me when she was twenty. My sister was born six years later." He smiled, twirling a curl of her hair around his finger as he spoke. "My dad trained a horse just for my mom, so she could ride even though she couldn't communicate with the horse through her legs. She ended up being an amazing barrel racer. To see her racing like that, fearless, was incredible. She was so free. My dad, God, if you could have seen my dad's face when he was watching her." He looked at Jaimi. "His entire world was focused around making her shine. I swore from early on that I wanted that, that I'd never settle for less."

Jaimi realized suddenly that he was talking in past tense about his parents, and her chest tightened. "What happened?"

His smile faded. "My mom's body had been damaged so much as a kid, that it eventually wore out. She died when I was eleven, and my sister was five."

"Oh, God. I'm so sorry." She reached out, setting her hand in his. "And your dad?"

He brought their joined hands to his lips and kissed them. "He was killed in a car accident a year later."

"Oh, *Dane*."

He nodded. "I visited him in the hospital after the accident. He was already in a coma, but I felt a huge sense of peace from him. I think he wanted to be with her."

Jaimi's gut tightened. "How could a dad choose to abandon his kids?"

"No." Dane held up his hand. "He didn't *choose* to abandon us. He *accepted* what fate had given him. There's a difference." He cocked his head. "It sounds like your mom was the same, wasn't she?"

Jaimi thought back to that last call she'd had with her mom, and how cheerful her mom had been, how insistent she'd been that Jaimi not be sad or live in regret. "You're right," she admitted. "That's exactly how she was the last time I spoke with her."

Dane nodded. "So, we get it, right? As kids, it sucks to be left behind, but we get it, right?"

"I guess." She sighed and sank deeper into the couch. "So, if you and your sister were so young, who raised you?" She sat up suddenly, fear knifing at her. "Not my father?"

"No. My mom's sister and her husband."

There was something in his tone that made her tense. "It wasn't good?"

He met her gaze. "My mom's sister felt like their parents had favored my mom because of her illness and physical challenges. My aunt was locked in a loveless marriage, without kids, and she bitterly resented the fact that my mom had somehow found a life of freedom, love, and motherhood, despite being in a wheelchair." He shrugged. "She hated me and my sister, and she made sure we knew it."

Sadness clogged Jaimi's throat at the thought of Dane losing his incredible parents, and then being thrust into a home where he was hated. "What was it like?"

He paused for a long moment, then shrugged. "It wasn't that different from what your brothers grew up with."

"Oh, *Dane*." Tears filled her eyes. "I'm so sorry."

"It's okay. The Stocktons protected me, and I protected them. We all became stronger because of it. They helped me keep my sister safe. If I was out of the house, one of the Stocktons, usually Ryder, would always be sleeping in her room, watching over her to make sure my uncle didn't pay her a visit during the night."

He didn't need to say more. She felt sick. "You protected her?"

"We all did, especially Ryder. He was fierce about it. My uncle never got to her. Not once. But we knew what he was like, and we were ready to do whatever it took. Hell, I turned down a free ride at college to take a deputy job so I could stay in town. There was no chance I was going to leave her behind."

So, that was how he'd ended up being sheriff. He'd taken the job so he could protect his sister, and that had become his life. No wonder she felt safe with him. He truly was a born protector.

Dane leaned in, searching her face. "I have to be honest with you, Jaimi. If my uncle had ever touched Zoey, he would have met the same fate as your father, and I would never have wasted a second regretting it."

She felt the truth in his voice, and in the hardness of his tone. He meant it. He would have killed his uncle if he'd harmed his sister. When he'd described what Chase had done to save Travis, it had horrified her. But now, hearing Dane talk about his sister, it felt different. She somehow understood now. "She was so lucky to have you."

He nodded. "I was lucky to have her, too. She was my only connection to our parents. I needed that reminder that there was good in this world." He sighed. "But we all lived in a constant state of tension until she was old enough to move out. The day she left town to go to college was the best damn day of my life." His smile faded. "I wanted everything for her," he said softly. "I wanted it all."

"It didn't work out?"

He sighed. "She has stuff going on right now. It's not good. I think she's moving back to town." He leaned forward and kissed Jaimi. "I don't want to talk about Zoey. I want to talk about us." He slid his hand along her jaw. "When you threw yourself at me when the tractor was coming, I finally understood what my dad had felt when he met my mom. When you know, you know."

Her heart started to pound. "How do you know?"

He set his hand over her heart. "Feel it there. Your heart speaks the truth, if you listen."

She closed her eyes and focused on the feel of his hand, on the warmth of his touch. The most incredible sense of peace and rightness filled her, so beautiful that she couldn't keep tears from filling her eyes. She opened her eyes. "Love," she whispered. "It feels like love."

He smiled. "That's because it is." He bent his head and kissed her, a beautiful, tender kiss that made her heart ache.

She slid her arms around his neck, kissing him back, losing herself in everything that he was. His tenderness. His kindness. His strength. His love. *His love.*

Maybe it didn't make sense for their bond to be so intense so quickly. Maybe it was illogical. But she knew that he was correct: this connection between them was special. "Dane?"

"Yeah?" He bent his head to nibble on her neck

"Would it be impossible for me to be falling in love with you so quickly?"

He looked down at her. "It would be impossible for you not to be. I'm freaking amazing."

She burst out laughing. "You're supposed to say that it's not impossible because you're falling in love with me, too."

"Am I?" With a low chuckle, he slid his arms beneath her and scooped her up against his chest. "I hate playing by the rules. It's not my thing." He stood up, cradling her as he began walking toward the one room in the house she hadn't yet been in.

His bedroom.

CHAPTER 18

*J*aimi's heart leapt. "Are you taking me to bed?"

"Yeah, you look tired." Dane carried her over the threshold, kissing her as he kicked the door shut and then locked it. "You need some sleep, hon." He set her on the bed and stood back. "Sleep well. I'll just camp out on the couch."

She propped herself up on her elbows, watching as he strode over to the dresser and began unbuttoning his shirt. "You're getting undressed in here?"

"Yeah, it's my bedroom. I do that kind of thing in here." He pulled off his shirt, revealing ripped abs and shoulders that made her want to whimper. "You don't mind, do you?"

"No, not at all. I'm always up for a little eye candy." She rolled onto her stomach and propped her chin up on her hands, making a show of ogling him. "Can you show me more?"

He grinned, shooting her a look of pure, decadent mischief. "Hell, yeah, baby. I'm a complete exhibitionist when the woman I love is stretched out on my bed."

"The woman you love?" Her heart leapt. "You just slipped

121

that in there, didn't you? Super casual, so that I could either ignore it, or acknowledge it."

Dane walked over to the bed, braced his hands on it and bent down, laying a super hot kiss on her. "Sweetheart, if you ignored it, it would've broken my poor li'l heart into a million pieces."

She sighed, grinning up at him as he stood up and ditched his boots and unfastened his belt buckle. "You have such a kind heart. I'd feel really bad if I broke it into a million pieces, or even just two."

"Now that, my dear, is the kind of thing I like to hear you say." He unfastened his jeans, and dropped them to the floor, revealing a lean, hard body with muscular quads, and black boxer briefs that clung to him in the most delicious of ways.

Her belly tightened, and her body suddenly seemed to catch fire. "You're way hot."

"I know." He strode over to the bed and grabbed her ankles, rolling her onto her back. "You're breathtaking."

She giggled as he leaned her feet against his chest and began to unlace her boots. "I know."

He tossed the boots aside, and then eyed her. "Do you always sleep fully clothed?"

"No. I usually wear pajama pants and a tank top." Her heart raced as she waited for him to make the next move.

He pursed his lips as if he were thinking. "Do you feel like going out into the living room to get your suitcase?"

"Not at all. You?"

"Nah. I'm not feeling chivalrous right now, and since it's all about both of us following our hearts, I say that we skip the clothes and just sleep naked. It feels like too much effort to put pajamas on."

Her heart began to pound. "You said you were sleeping on the couch."

"I know. But again, it feels like a lot of effort to go all the way out there." He let her feet drop so that one was on either side of his hips. Then he leaned over her, bracing his hands on either side of her head. "What do you say to some innocent, platonic, naked co-sleeping?" He lowered himself just enough to begin to nibble on her neck.

She sighed. "No."

"No?" He grabbed the hem of her shirt and tugged gently. She raised her arms over her head and let him tug it off. He paused to kiss along the swell of her breasts. The tender, flirty kisses were so intimate, the kind of intimate that was about so much more than sex. "Then, what do you say to me doing my best to convince you that I'm your forever guy, in every way possible?"

She caught her breath, her hands resting on his biceps. "Forever is a long time."

He pulled back to look at her. "Forever isn't even close to being long enough." He didn't give her a chance to answer. He just kissed her, the kind of kiss that went straight to her heart and nestled deep inside, taking root in the place that she had never let anything touch before.

He whispered her name and sank onto the bed beside her, pulling her into his arms as he kissed her. She had no chance to resist, and she didn't want to. All she wanted was to give herself over to him completely. Not just her body, but her heart, and her mind.

He palmed her breast as he kissed his way along her neck, stoking fires in her that had never been even a spark before she'd met him. The kisses became more intense. The touches became more vivid, and more desperate. Before she was even aware of it happening, suddenly there were no more clothes between them, just bare skin, kisses, and the kind of tender, intimate touches that brought light into her heart, light that ignited a need that seemed to pulsate through her.

She wrapped her arms around Dane's neck, kissing him

fiercely as his fingers slipped between her legs, stoking need in her that was delicious and decadent, spiraling tighter and tighter.

Her body moved against him, calling for him, begging for more, as he kept teasing her with his kisses, his touches, and his whispers of intimacy and love. "Dane," she finally whispered. "I can't wait anymore."

He pulled back, his eyes dark with the most possessive and electrifying light in his eyes. "Yes." He leaned away from her, grabbed something from his drawer, and quickly sheathed himself in a condom. He was back over her quickly, but not soon enough, not soon enough for how badly she needed him inside her.

He braced himself above her, gazing down into her face as he began to move his hips, nudging at her entrance. "Jaimi." His voice was husky and low, making her belly tighten.

"What?" She gasped as he began to slide inside her, so delicious and amazing that she almost wanted to cry.

"You need to know something." He shifted his hips again, and then he was completely inside her.

She arched her back, gasping as he began to move. "What do I need to know?"

He paused, and she opened her eyes to look at him. "I give you my heart forever, Jaimi. It's yours. If you walk away from here tomorrow and go back to Boston, you will have my heart with you, keeping you safe, loving you, every minute of every day for the rest of forever."

Tears filled her eyes, and suddenly she couldn't talk.

He smiled gently, and bent down to kiss her. "Now that I've found you, we have all the time in the world," he said softly. "It's okay if you're not ready. I'll hold us together until you are. Let me be your rock. Yours and Emily's."

Emily's. The way he said her daughter's name, with such

complete protectiveness, made the tears break free. "She doesn't know what it's like to have a dad."

He smiled. "I think we might do okay. What do you think?"

She nodded. "I think you guys might do just fine," she acknowledged.

His face softened. "My sweet Jaimi." He kissed her again, driving deep as he kissed her, until she could do nothing but hold on and ride the waves he'd stoked inside her. The orgasm came like a burst of sunshine in a storm, cascading through her like droplets of angel dust, taking them both in a simultaneous blaze of flight.

She held tight to him, using him as her anchor as the final shudders echoed through her body, her eyes squeezed shut as he kissed the tears off her cheeks.

Forever was a long time.

Love was a big word.

But somehow, as she lay wrapped in Dane's strong arms, they didn't feel so big, and they didn't feel so scary.

~

DANE WAS BASKING in the feel of Jaimi asleep on his shoulder when the first rays of light broke through the morning haze. He grinned, playing with her hair as he listened to her breathing. He'd checked on Emily three times during the night, and the little girl had slept soundly, holding Zoey's old teddy bear, which he'd found in the closet for her.

He inhaled deeply. God, he'd never felt so at peace in his life. For the first time since his parents had died, his home felt like a home. With Jaimi in his arms, and Emily in the next room, there was completeness.

He knew he had to deal with the Stocktons today, and all he'd done was shoot Chase a quick text last night that he'd found Jaimi and brought them back to his house. He was going to have to find a way to bridge that gap.

But right now, today, he didn't want to.

He wanted today to be about the three of them, beginning to build the trust and foundation that he wanted with them. He knew Jaimi was scared, but he also knew that she'd opened the door for him. She'd given him a piece of her heart, and he was going to make damn sure he kept it safe—

"Hello! Anyone here?" Chase's voice boomed from the front door, jerking Dane out of his reverie.

He bolted upright in bed, as Jaimi mumbled sleepily. What the hell was Chase doing there? "I'll be right back, love. You can keep sleeping." He kissed Jaimi, and was rewarded when she opened her eyes and gave him a sleepy smile.

"Kiss me again," she mumbled.

"So demanding," he said with a grin as he took a moment to accommodate her, trying not to listen to the sounds coming from his living room. There was too much noise and clattering for just Chase. What was going on out there? "Okay, love, I need to go do some exterminating," he said. "I'll be right back."

"Okay." She rolled over and closed her eyes, nestling deeper into the blankets.

Dane vaulted out of bed, yanking on his clothes in record speed. He paused at the door, looking back at her in his bed. A sense of absolute rightness filled him, and he was smiling as he opened the door.

Then he took one look at what was in his living room, and all his amusement vanished.

CHAPTER 19

*C*hristmas had come to his house, and it had brought elves. Elves with Stockton eyes, cheekbones, cowboy hats, wives, and kids. "What the hell is going on?"

Chase looked over from the corner, where he and Ryder were installing a Christmas tree in a stand. "What does it look like we're doing?"

"Putting up a Christmas tree in my living room."

"So, why ask, then? You got it." Chase turned away, angling the tree as Mira directed the men on which way to lean the tree to get it straight.

Travis and Lissa were in the kitchen, and he could see them unpacking boxes. He could see three pies on the counter already, plus three cartons of eggs, and fresh bread. The front door opened again, and Zane walked in with his two boys, all of them carrying cardboard boxes with red and green Christmas decorations overflowing from the top.

Ava, Hannah and Maddox's daughter, was at the coffee table with Bridgette, Lissa and Travis's daughter. The two of them had three Christmas stockings on the table, and an assortment of glitter glue, sparkles and felt letters. He could see the start of Emily and Jaimi's name on them, and realized the girls were making Christmas stockings for the three of them, which was incredibly thoughtful.

Maddox was on a stepstool, nailing Christmas lights around the perimeter of his walls, up by the ceiling, while Erin and Taylor were camped out at his fireplace, turning his mantle into a Christmas bonanza.

"Hey!" Dane held up his hands to try to quiet the din, but no one really listened. "Why are you setting up Christmas in my house?"

Mira put her hands on her hips and turned to face him. "Dane, you may not have noticed that you haven't had a single Christmas decoration in your house in all the years I've known you, but I noticed it. It's sad, and I tried to fix it by having you at our house for Christmas, but I always hated the idea of you coming home to a house with no Christmas spirit."

He blinked, startled by her comment. "You did?" He glanced at Chase, who grinned and shrugged.

"Yes." Mira set her hands on her hips. "And I was lying in bed last night, and the thought of Jaimi and Emily having to spend even a single day of the Christmas season without Christmas spirit was just so wrong. So, I woke Chase up, and he agreed."

Dane shot a look at Chase, who grinned. "It was three in the morning. I would have agreed to anything at that hour, and she knows it."

"So, I called everyone this morning," Mira continued, "and we all rounded up whatever spare decorations we could find, and agreed to bring them over." She grinned innocently. "So, here we are. Bringing you the Christmas you have deserved for so long."

He folded his arms over his chest. "This isn't for me. It's for them."

"No." Mira walked over to him and pressed a kiss to his cheek. "It's for all of you. You're just as deserving as they are, but yes, I admit, it took having a new sister-in-law and niece to get me to take action."

Dane grimaced, glancing at his closed bedroom door. "They don't know you know," he warned. "I promised her I wouldn't tell."

Mira winked. "I know. So, you'll have to figure out how to explain us." Without another word, she walked off, asking Lissa and Travis how long it would be until breakfast was ready.

"Breakfast?" Dane echoed. "You guys are eating here?"

"Yep." Lissa waved at him from the kitchen. "We're all staying for breakfast with Jaimi and Emily. We want to know the woman who has won your heart."

Hell. Dane stood there, completely ignored and powerless as the Stocktons took over his house. He knew there was no way he was getting them out of there. "Doesn't anyone in this family know how long forty-eight hours is?"

"Sorry," Maddox said as he set a box down. "None of us know how to tell time. It's a Stockton thing."

"And it affects us when we marry them," Taylor chimed in. "It's kind of weird." She grinned at him. "Smile, Dane. You can't stop us."

As Dane stood there, watching the Stocktons turn his house into a Christmas oasis, a part of him wanted to grin, grab a strand of tinsel, and join right in. The other part of him was scared shitless about how Jaimi would react if she walked out and found them there.

Swearing, he walked over to Chase. "Can we talk?"

Chase handed him a string of lights. "We can talk while we put lights on the tree."

Dane swore and took the strand. "Chase, you don't get it. She's running scared. She's ready to go back to Boston today.

She's terrified of the blood that runs in her veins now. She was reluctant to tell you guys who she was in the first place, but now she's scared shitless." He grabbed Chase's arm. "I can't lose her, Chase. I need her in my life."

Chase paused to look at him, then set down the lights. "Outside."

The two men navigated quickly around the mess and walked out into the snowy morning. It was bright, snowy, and cold as hell. Dane hugged his arms to his chest as he faced Chase, wishing he'd grabbed a coat. "I'm asking you to leave, Chase. It's too much of a risk."

Chase met his gaze. "She's my sister, Dane. I'm not walking away from her."

"You *have* to."

Chase ground his jaw for a moment, then shook his head. "Did you see who was in your house this morning?"

"Yeah, of course."

"Did you see who wasn't?"

Dane frowned. "What do you mean?"

"Who was missing? Who should have been here?"

He realized what Chase was talking about. "Caleb, Logan, and Quintin." The three Stockton brothers who hadn't yet reclaimed their roots.

"Yeah. Only six of us are here. We don't even know where Caleb is. He's gone. Missing. I don't even know if he's alive." Pain flashed in Chase's eyes. "Every one of my brothers left town, Dane. You and I were the only ones here for years. They'd stop by, but everyone had walked away from the memories. I tried to hold the family together by giving them all the space to walk away, and I thought I'd lost them all by doing it."

Dane and Chase had talked about it during those years. He knew how hard it had been on Chase, because the man was all about family. Nothing else mattered to him. Hell, he'd bought the Stockton ranch for the sole purpose of creating a homestead for his brothers to join him on. No one had come. Not one. Until they'd met the women who had drawn them home.

"I don't know if I will ever hear from Caleb again. I don't know if I'll even know what happened to him. If he died. If he's alive. He's just gone." He spread his hands. "My own brother. Lost to me, completely. Just like Jaimi. She's my sister, and I didn't even know she existed, Dane. *I didn't even know.*"

Dane sighed. "I know. I'm trying to bring her back to you, but it's not easy."

"I know it's not easy." Chase met his gaze. "I've been trying to get my brothers back for years. I know damn well how difficult it is. Logan and Quintin aren't coming back for Christmas. I don't know what they're doing, but they're not going to be here."

"I'm sorry, Chase. I know that sucks."

Chase put his hand on Dane's shoulder. "Look at me, bro. Look me in the eye and tell me that you are absolutely certain that if Jaimi walks away without resolving this, that she'll be back. That we all won't lose her forever."

Dane ground his jaw. "I can't. I don't know that she'd come back."

"Exactly." Chase let go of him. "One thing I've learned over the years is that if you love someone, you can't ever give up on them. Rivers of pain become uncrossable oceans that can't be bridged if you don't try to fix them when they're small. I'm lucky as hell that Travis, Steen, Zane, and Maddox found women who helped them heal, because I couldn't do it. But I learned my lesson. There's no way that I can let Jaimi walk away until I've done everything possible to bridge that gap. She's my *sister*, Dane."

"And she's the woman I love."

131

The two men stared at each other. "One doesn't trump the other," Chase said quietly. "They're both important."

Dane ground his jaw, trying to keep his voice even. "Yes, but she's afraid of you, and she's falling in love with me. I'm the one she trusts. You're the one who's going to make her run."

"So, let's make her unafraid."

Dane ran his hand through his hair. "I'm trying, but it's a little hard to do if you're here."

"Could you walk away from her if I asked you to?"

"Hell no—"

"Well, I can't walk away from her either, Dane. Don't ask me to do it, because it's impossible, both for me and my brothers. We all need her, because she's family." Chase set his hand on Dane's shoulder. "Let's do this together, Dane, like we used to as kids. We've gotten through the darkest of places together. We know how to make it work."

Dane swore. "If we fuck it up, the cost is too great."

"I know." Chase met his gaze. "Trust me, I know."

Dane sighed, hearing the seriousness of Chase's voice. "Yeah," he said. "I believe you do. So, what do we do?"

Chase grinned, relief evident in his eyes. "You're the one she's falling in love with," he said, with just a hint of amused challenge in his voice. "If you're worthy of my sister, and I'm not sure you are, then you're the one who has to know what she needs."

Dane glared at him. "You know I'm worthy of her. Don't be an ass."

"Just because you're worthy of being my brother, doesn't mean you're worthy of dating my sister. You gotta prove yourself. So, figure out how to fix it. We'll follow your lead, except, of course, if it involves any of us vacating."

Dane rolled his eyes. "Heaven forbid I suggest something sensible like that."

"Fuck sensibility. Be more creative than that." Chase grinned. "But you better think fast, because I can't imagine she's still asleep. At any second, she's going to walk out of your bedroom door, and you better have something figured out." He doffed his hat. "Good luck, bro." Then he turned and walked back into Dane's house, leaving Dane standing outside in his shirtsleeves.

Dane sighed and clasped his hands above his head. "The Stocktons are a bunch of bastards," he muttered.

"I heard that!" Chase yelled from inside.

Dane grinned. "You deserved it!"

"Love you, too, bro. Now fix it."

Fix it.

How the hell was he going to do that?

CHAPTER 20

*J*aimi sat on the edge of Dane's bed, her hands shaking, his comforter wrapped around her.

The Stocktons had invaded Dane's house. She could hear the conversation, the voices, the laughter, the noise. Chase's voice. Zane's. Travis's. Others she couldn't recognize yet.

What where they doing there? Why? Did they know she was there? Had they come to find her?

No, they couldn't have. They didn't know she was their sister. Dane had promised, and she trusted him.

So, she could go out there, and pretend to be sociable. Grab Emily and their luggage, and then sneak out the back door. Run for home before they knew the truth.

But as she sat there, she couldn't make herself move to get dressed. She was paralyzed with inaction. Terrified to face them. Afraid of having her heart broken if she walked out there, saw her *family*, and left them behind forever. But she was equally terrified of going out there, announcing who she was, and becoming a part of something that had so much darkness in it, something she had no idea how to belong to, even if she wasn't afraid of it.

"I don't belong with them," she whispered.

It didn't feel right.

"I belong with them," she tried again.

That didn't feel right either.

"I belong with Emily."

Yes, that felt good.

"I belong with Dane."

Tears filled her eyes, agonizing tears, because she knew it was true...but she knew it could never happen. She pressed her palms to her eyes, fighting off tears, wishing her mom was still alive, wishing that she had someone to ask for advice, someone who would tell her what was right.

But there was no one.

～

DANE HAD JUST STEPPED inside his living room when he saw Emily peek around the corner of the living room, her eyes wide. She was wearing footie pajamas with Christmas trees on them, and a long-sleeved top that said, "Girl Power," on it, with a badass female superhero on the front.

He quickly walked across the room to intercept her. "Hey, Em."

She looked up at him, and quickly gestured for him to come over to her. He grinned and went down on one knee, so he was at her level. "What's up, sweetie?"

"They're here."

"I know."

"Why?"

"They wanted to bring Christmas to us."

Emily looked past him, her eyes tracking rapidly as she scanned the room. "Why?"

He took a deep breath. "Because they thought we all deserved it."

She looked up at him. "Did they bring presents?"

He laughed. "Christmas isn't for a couple days. No presents until then."

"Oh." She looked so crestfallen that he almost laughed.

"But I'm sure there will be lots of presents."

"A horse?" She looked hopefully at him. "I want to learn how to barrel race, like the picture on my dresser."

Dane realized there was a photo of his mom on the night-stand in the room Emily was sleeping in, and his heart tightened at the thought of Emily following the path of his mom. He knew he'd feel just as much pride watching her as his dad had experienced watching the woman he'd loved. "You'd make a great barrel racer. My mom used to barrel race. She loved it."

"Really?" Emily stared at him. "Can you teach me?"

"Yeah, I could."

"Will you?"

Dane glanced at his closed bedroom door. "We'd have to check with your mom, first."

Emily sighed. "She'll say no. Can you smack down her inner wimp?"

He burst out laughing at the phrase that Emily had used before. "Smack down her inner wimp, eh?"

"Yeah, Grandma says that mommy's inner wimp is a ruth-less bully and needs a smackdown." Emily searched his face. "Dane?"

"Yeah, sweetie."

"Mommy's going to make us leave today. I don't want to leave."

He sighed. "I don't want you to leave either."

"I don't want to be a spy anymore." She looked past him. "They're so nice," she whispered, in a whisper loud enough that the whole room could hear. And hear they did, because he'd suddenly noticed that everyone had stopped talking. They were all still ostensibly engaged in their Christmas tasks, but they were working in absolute silence. He could practically see them all bending toward their corner of the living room, listening to him and Emily talk.

The Stocktons might want to hug their sister, but their hearts were just as desperate to welcome their niece, and he knew they would protect her with everything they had, just as they'd taken care of Zoey. Emily needed them. Every kid in the world would be better off with the Stocktons at their back.

Dane grinned. "They think you're amazing," he whispered back. "They love you already."

Emily's eyes widened. "Really?" She looked so in awe, so happy, so stunned that his chest tightened. "I love them," she whispered, again, loud enough that everyone present could hear.

Dane glanced over his shoulder and saw Chase grinning. Mira was wiping tears off her cheeks, and little Ava was staring at Emily with wide eyes.

Shit. He wanted to tell Emily the truth, that the Stocktons already knew she was family, and wanted her and Jaimi to be a part of their lives. He really did. But he couldn't betray Jaimi any more than he already had—

"Emily?" Ava sidled up next to Dane and leaned against him, facing Emily.

Emily got a shy look on her face. "Hi."

"Is it true you're my cousin?"

Fuck. He looked back at Maddox, but Ava's dad was pretending to look at the ceiling. Son of a bitch.

Emily looked at Dane, then back at Ava, longing etched on her face. "I'm not supposed to tell," she whispered loudly. "I'm a spy."

Ava grinned. "I like spies. Can I be a spy, too?"

"I don't know." She looked at Dane. "Can Ava be a spy, too? Or is it just me and my mom?"

"I think she can be a spy," Dane said, hoping to redirect the conversation away from family and toward top-secret codes instead.

"Cool!" Emily grinned. "If you're a spy, too, then I can tell you all my spy secrets."

Oh, *shit.* He hadn't seen that coming. "Emily—"

"My mom is Chase's sister, and all the others. And you're my cousin. I've never had cousins. It's cool, right?"

"Cousins!" Ava whirled around. "Mom! Emily's my cousin!" she bellowed. "You were right! Can we have a sleepover?"

Dane looked at his bedroom door, only a few feet from Ava, and his gut sank. There was no chance that Jaimi hadn't heard that, and he heard from the groans that every adult in the room had come to the same conclusion. He looked helplessly at Chase.

"You better go in and talk to her," Chase said to him. "Come on, ladies." He scooped up the two little girls, one in each arm. "Let's go see if Lissa's chocolate chip muffins are almost ready." With Ava and Emily still chattering loudly about being cousins, he carried them into the kitchen.

Dane bowed his head for a long moment, resting his elbow on his knee. He had no idea how to fix this, but he knew that if he got it wrong, he was going to lose everything that mattered to him.

In the few seconds he stayed there, no solutions came to him. He had no fucking idea how to save this. None.

But he knew his time was up, so without looking at anyone else, he rose to his feet, walked to his bedroom, and put his hand on the knob. He paused to take a deep breath, and then opened the door and walked in.

CHAPTER 21

When Dane walked in and saw the stricken look on Jaimi's face, he knew that he was almost too late. She was sitting on the end of his bed, his comforter pulled so tightly around her that he wasn't sure he could ever get her free of it. She stared at him wordlessly, terrified, shocked, confused.

He shut the door. "Hey."

Hey. What an asinine thing to say. But he literally had no idea what to say. He was too terrified of screwing it up. He realized that his hands were shaking as well, and he felt like he could barely breathe.

"They know," she whispered. "I heard. They know."

"Yeah." He walked across the room and knelt in front of her, setting his hands on her hips. "They figured it out last night. You both look too much like Stocktons."

"You said they wouldn't know. You said it would be okay."

"I was wrong." He could feel her trembling, and somehow, that made his tension fade. She was afraid. She needed him right now. She needed him to be strong for them both.

"Make them leave," she whispered. "Make them go away."

139

He paused, a thousand possible responses whirling through his brain. Things she wanted to hear. Things she needed to hear. Things he thought would be smart to say. Things that might work. Things that weren't his truth, the truth that his heart was telling him to say.

So, he spoke from the heart. "I love you, Jaimi."

She stared at him and shook her head. "No, don't say that. I need to leave—"

"No, you don't." He slid his hands under the comforter, moving them until he found her hands. They were ice cold and trembling. "I love you, and I love your kid. You know that, right?"

Her fingers tightened around his even as she shook her head. "Don't—"

"You know what love means to me. I told you about my parents. You understand what drives me, and how I operate, right?"

She swallowed and nodded silently.

"You know what family means to me, right? How I protected my sister? How I gave up a life outside this town because she needed me, right?"

She nodded again. "You're a protector," she whispered, her gaze flicking past him to the door, where the low hum of whispered conversation had resumed again.

"Exactly. I protect those I love fiercely, and that means you."

Her gaze flicked back to him. "You love them, as well. The Stocktons. You love them."

"I do, but they're my brothers. I'm stuck with them." He slid his hands to her face, loosening the comforter enough to frame her face. "But you, I *choose*." He kissed her gently, offering his strength to her cold lips.

She grasped his wrists, bent her head, resting her forehead against his chin. "I can't do this."

He began to play with her hair. "Last night, when I came back to look for you after you ditched me on the trailer—"

She looked up. "I ditched you because you made me leave my daughter with a murderer!"

"No." He put his finger over her lips. "Not a murderer. Never a murderer. Self-defense, or defense of others is not murder. It's survival." He sighed as she tensed, quickly resuming his story before they could get bogged down in that issue. He had a plan to deal with that in a moment. "When I walked over there, they were all standing there, challenging me, demanding to know about you. They knew that you and Emily were related to them, but they didn't know how. When I told them, do you know what they said?"

She shook her head, staring at him.

"I asked them not to go after you, and Chase told me that you were his sister, and he wasn't going to wait. He wanted to meet you *as his sister*." He cupped her face in his hands. "They love you already," he said gently. "Chase took me outside this morning when I told him they had to leave, and he told me that he wasn't going to give up on you. He needed you. They all need you. In their hearts, you became family the moment they found out you existed."

Tears filled her eyes and spilled out over her cheeks. "Really?"

"Really." He took a breath, and took one more risk, raising his voice. "Travis? Can you come in here?"

Jaimi tensed as the door opened immediately, as if someone had been listening at the door, which didn't surprise Dane in the least. He glanced over his shoulder as Travis walked in, and shut the door behind him, but not before Dane got a glimpse of everyone peering in, trying to see what was going on.

Jaimi caught her breath. "I'm naked under this," she hissed to Dane.

Travis grinned. "Trust me, I don't need to see my sister naked. I'm not peeking."

Jaimi pulled the comforter tighter around her. "You're an ass, Dane."

"I know." He sat next to Jaimi on the bed and put his arm around her. "Travis, show her the scar from your dad."

The smile dropped off Travis's face. "Seriously?"

"Yeah."

Jaimi made a small noise of protest. "I don't need to see this."

"Yes, you do." Dane gestured at Travis. "Show her the scar. Tell her what happened."

Travis stared at Dane for a long moment, and then began to unbutton his shirt. "I was a skinny teenager," he said, his voice even, devoid of emotion as he began to talk. "My dad was a piece of shit bastard."

The door opened, and Lissa slipped inside, and closed the door behind her. She walked up to Travis and slid her arms around his waist, holding him as he spoke. Travis sighed deeply when she touched him, and he shot her a grateful smile, displaying the same kind of love Dane used to see on his dad's face.

"I was the youngest," Travis continued, as he resumed unbuttoning his shirt. "My older brothers did a hell of a job protecting me, but eventually, I was the only one who still lived at home. One night, my dad came back from a night of drinking. I was in the garage playing guitar. I had the door locked from the inside, which I always did when he was out drinking."

He finished unbuttoning his shirt, and left it hanging open. Jaimi couldn't help but look at his torso, wondering what was hiding beneath it. She didn't want to know. She really didn't. But she was rooted in place, not just because she was naked and Dane's arm was around her, but because something deeper was calling her to this man, her brother, this famous superstar who was her own brother.

"My dad wanted to fight, and I ignored him. He started banging on the door, yelling at me to let him in." Travis put his arm around Lissa, and kissed the top of her head. The expression on Lissa's face was pure, unconditional, beautiful love, exactly how Dane had been looking at Jaimi right before he'd called Travis in.

"I went quiet," Travis said, "hoping he'd leave. He always wore himself out and left eventually. But this time, he didn't. He had a gun."

Jaimi sat up, almost losing her comforter before Dane pulled it tighter around her. "A gun? He was going to *shoot* you?"

"I don't know. He started shooting the door, and one of the bullets almost hit me. I had no way out, so I grabbed a shovel and opened the door."

Jaimi held her breath. "What happened?"

"He came at me like a lunatic. I got one blow in with the shovel, and then he pulled out his switchblade. He stabbed me." As he spoke, Travis pulled his shirt to the side. On his torso were several long scars across his stomach and ribs. Four scars. "The stab wounds weren't the problem. He broke my ribs and one of them punctured my lung. He left me on the floor and locked me in. I could feel my lungs filling up, and I knew I needed to get to the hospital fast, but I was locked in."

"Oh, God," she whispered, unable to stop the tears.

"Tell her the rest," Dane said, his voice rough with emotion. "Tell her what Chase did."

Jaimi finally understood what Dane was doing. He was trying to show her what her brothers were really like. "I don't—"

"Yes, you do." Dane said firm. "Travis, finish it."

Travis pulled his shirt closed over his chest and sat down on an armchair in the corner of Dane's room. Lissa sat down sideways on his lap, her arms wrapped around him as he spoke. Travis locked his arms around her waist, holding tightly. "I called Chase. I told him to get me out of there."

She glanced at Dane. "You didn't call the police?"

"Dane wasn't sheriff then. The sheriff at the time was a drinking buddy of my dad's. Things weren't right in this town until Dane took over." He glanced at Dane. "We needed you."

"You got me now. I'm not going anywhere." He squeezed Jaimi. "See? Everyone loves me."

She managed a smile as Travis resumed his story. "When Chase showed up, my dad met him with a gun. Told him to walk away. Chase didn't. He went for the garage to get me out, and my dad went after him. They fought, and my dad ended up dead." He met Jaimi's gaze. "And that was the day we all became free."

Silence fell, and Jaimi couldn't stop the tears. "I'm so sorry."

"I'm not. He needed to die." Travis pressed a kiss to Lissa's hair, while she ran her hand over his arm, clearly comforting him. "But here's the thing, Jaimi, the thing we've all had to understand. That bastard might be the man who fathered all of us, including you, but he's nothing to us. He's a past that we share, but we'll never let him win. None of us have ever touched a drink in our lives. None of us have ever touched anyone in anger, let alone a child or a woman. And we never will. He didn't win, Jaimi. He didn't beat us, and he's not going to stand in the way of us finding our sister."

Jaimi suddenly felt deep shame for what she'd thought of them, for how she'd judged them. She'd believed in Dane, even when he'd admitted he would have killed his uncle to protect his sister, but she'd refused to give that same treatment to her brothers.

How much they had all suffered, and yet somehow, they were all upstanding, loyal, family men. Dads. Husbands. Siblings. Good people.

"Thanks, Travis," Dane said.

Her brother nodded. "I don't talk about that night, Jaimi. I wouldn't tell that story for anyone, except my sister."

"Thank you for trusting me," she said quietly, her throat raw.

"You bet."

Lissa tapped Travis's arm. "Let's give them a moment."

Travis looked like he was going to argue, then sighed when Lissa raised her eyebrows at him. They both stood up. "We'll be in the living room," Travis said. "We're getting hungry. Don't make us wait long for breakfast, sis."

He winked at her as he took Lissa's hand and followed her out the door.

The door shut behind them, leaving her alone with Dane.

For a long moment, they sat in silence. Jaimi leaned into Dane, and closed her eyes, focusing on the strength and warmth of his frame as he held her. "That was mean," she finally said.

"Mean?"

"Yes. How am I supposed to continue to judge and resist my brothers when I see them in that light?"

He made a strangled noise, and suddenly she found herself on her back, with Dane bracing himself on his forearms above her. "Damn, woman, don't ever mess with me like that again. I was scared shitless walking in here, wondering how I could possibly keep from losing you. Having Travis tell his story was all I could think of, but the whole time he was talking, I kept thinking that maybe I'd done the one thing that would make me lose you forever."

She saw the tension in his eyes, and felt the depth of his fear. "I didn't know it would work either," she admitted. "I didn't want to hear it, but I needed to." She locked her hands behind Dane's neck, needing to feel him against her. "The story helped me understand Chase, but it scared me about my dad."

He nodded. "I knew it would. I'm sorry."

She smiled, her heart softening at the tenderness in Dane's face. "But when I saw how Lissa looked at Travis, how much she loves him and trusts him, I knew that there was beauty in his soul. That somehow, someway, he, and the others, have managed to be good people despite their dad." She paused. "Our dad." *Our dad.* The words sounded so foreign. Both words. Sharing a parent with someone else. And having a father. "I would wish that I didn't have a horrible man for a father, but my mom would be so not impressed that I just said that."

Dane grinned. "Let me guess. She'd tell you to appreciate the fact you have nine brothers, five sisters-in-law, and a whole slew of nieces and nephews."

"Undoubtedly." Jaimi searched Dane's face, and her own heart. "She'd also have something else to say."

His brows went up. "What's that?"

"She'd be utterly disappointed in me if I gave up the greatest adventure of my life because I was afraid."

He smiled. "And what adventure is that, my love?"

"Loving you." She took a deep breath, surprised at how liberating and beautiful it sounded to admit that aloud. "I love you, Dane. My heart loves you." She put her hand on his chest, over his heart. "My soul is at peace when I'm with you. My mom always said that our greatest, most reliable compass is nestled deep in our souls. And it's pointing to you."

His smile widened. "The most beautiful words I've ever

heard," he whispered. "Forever won't be enough time, but we'll have to take it. I love you, Jaimi, and we're just getting started." He bent his head and kissed her, the most sensual, most amazing, most loving kiss of her life—

A loud knock sounded on the door. "Just in case you forget," Lissa called out. "Your bedroom door is unlocked, and there are two young spies out here who aren't going to wait much longer before they drag you two out here for breakfast."

Jaimi giggled as Dane let out a low groan and buried his face in her neck. "Five minutes. All I want is five minutes with the woman I love. Is that so much to ask?"

She grinned. "Well, we don't have five minutes. Would forever work instead?"

He lifted his head. "Forever is a big word," he teased gently.

"It is."

He grinned. "It kinda scares me."

She laughed as he played her old sentiments back to her. "Well, it's a good thing that I'm badass and brave. I'll keep us together until you're ready to handle me."

"That's fantastic." He kissed her hard and deep, then pulled back. "Not that I don't like you naked in a comforter, but I'm wondering if maybe it will be hard to eat breakfast that way."

She raised her eyebrows. "You think jeans?"

"And a shirt." He pulled the comforter aside and inspected her bare chest. He kissed each breast twice, then nodded. "Yes, definitely a shirt."

"God, there are such weird customs in Wyoming." She pushed him off her and grabbed her bra from the floor where they'd tossed it the night before. "I can't believe naked family breakfasts aren't a thing."

He lounged back on the bed, watching her with a heated

gaze as she got dressed. "We could make it a thing. Send Emily over to Hannah and Maddox's for a cousin sleepover, and then do a naked breakfast with just us."

"With strawberries and whipped cream?"

"Hell, yeah." He paused. "I assume you mean that I am supposed to lick the whipped cream off you?"

Finished with her clothes, she sat next to him to put on her boots, her soul emitting a deep sigh of peace when he set his hand on her back. "No, that would just be sticky and messy. We would just eat. We've made love once, why do we need to do it again?"

"Why?" He grabbed her around the waist and tossed her back on the bed. "*Why?*" He lowered himself on her and kissed her fiercely, until she was a puddle of melted goo. He pulled back. "That's why."

"Oh." She wrinkled her brow. "That's a good reason. I'm in."

"Thank God. And the whipped cream?"

She grinned. "I'll consider it as a definite possibility."

"Awesome. That's all I ask, is for you to consider it." Dane swung off the bed and held out his hand, pulling her to her feet when she settled her hand in his. "Ready?"

"Not even close."

"Great. Nothing good ever waits until you're ready." He wrapped his arms around her, enveloping her in a tight hug. "I love you, sweetheart. I'm in this with you."

"I know." She hugged him back, wishing she could stay in his arms forever. "My mom would love you," she whispered. "You make me brave."

"My parents would have loved you. You're everything that I deserve."

She laughed and swatted his chest. "What about me?"

"I'm everything you deserve." He grinned and caught her wrist as she swatted at him again. "Quick question before we go out there. Are you still planning to go back to Boston today?"

She took a deep breath. "No."

"Tomorrow?"

She shook her head. "I'm kind of keeping it open-ended right now."

He walked them toward the door. "Can I make a request?"

"Sure." Her heart started to race as he reached for the door.

"Stay forever. With me. With your family. With all of us." He paused with his hand on the knob. "When you're ready, I'm going to ask you to marry me. It's going to be extremely romantic, so it'll be worth staying around for."

She swallowed. "I'm beginning to like romance."

He grinned. "So, you'll think about it?"

She squeezed his hand. "I'll definitely consider it."

"Fantastic." His smile faded. "You've got this."

She looked into his eyes, into his handsome face, so full of love, and she knew he was right. She did have it.

The door suddenly opened. "Mom?"

She smiled at her daughter. "Yes, pumpkin?"

"They know."

Her smile widened. "I know."

"So, we don't have to be spies?"

"Nope."

"Not ever?"

"Not ever." As she spoke, Jaimi glanced out in the living room. The first person she saw was Chase, who was leaning against the far wall, watching her. Tears filled her eyes, and suddenly she couldn't talk.

Chase immediately levered himself off the wall and strode across the room toward her. Dane put his hand on her back as Chase approached, and she leaned into him, her heart racing as Chase neared.

He stopped just in front of her, his blue eyes twinkling. "Hey, sis. Welcome to the family." His voice was thick with emotion, making her own tears spill free.

"I never wanted a brother," she whispered.

He grinned. "What are you going to do with nine of them, then?"

"Cry?"

"That works for me." He reached for her, and she instinctively moved forward, and then suddenly, she was being held in the tightest hug she'd ever had in her life. There was a resounding cheer, and then suddenly, more arms were being flung around her, until she was buried in hugs, loving arms, and tears of joy.

"Merry Christmas, sweetheart," Dane whispered in her ear, his arms locked around her waist, as he stood behind her, his body her shield, as she knew it always would be.

She looked over her shoulder at him and smiled. "Thank you," she whispered.

He kissed her cheek. "Forever starts today."

For the first time in her life, forever didn't scare her.

Forever with Dane, and her family, felt perfect.

CHAPTER 22

hristmas, One Year Later

"Mom! We're going to be late!" Emily bounced agitatedly in her booster seat, her face pressed up against the window of Dane's truck as he turned into Chase's driveway. "Drive faster, Dane! They're going to start without us!"

"We're not even opening presents until after dinner," Jaimi said, twisting awkwardly around in her seat to grin at her daughter. The Christmas lights on Chase and Mira's house were twinkling, and she could see the giant, inflatable reindeer and Santa lawn decorations through the trees. Apparently, the inflatables had come at the request of their toddler, J.J., who had decided that no horse ranch would be complete without gigantic inflatable Christmas decorations, and Chase had agreed.

She loved it.

She loved everything about the Christmas season with the Stocktons. Christmas cookie baking with Lissa and the kids. Communal present-wrapping with homemade cookies and pies while the kids were having snowball fights. Going shopping with Erin and Taylor for Christmas decorations, and food for Christmas dinner.

And, most importantly, waking up every morning in Dane's arms, knowing that he was a part of her and Emily's life forever.

"Uh uh!" Emily protested. "Uncle Travis said that me and Ava could pick something first and open it right away. He said that he'd make sure we picked a good one!"

Dane grinned as he eased his truck along the snowy driveway. "Erin and Steen are behind us, so we're not the last ones."

"What?" Emily peered out the back window, and then waved frantically. "Aunt Erin is the best vet ever. I want to be a vet like her. Then I could take care of all our horses myself."

"*All* our horses?" Jaimi rolled her eyes. "We just have one."

"For now! Ava said that all the cowgirls have more than one barrel racer. When I get good enough, I'm going to need more!"

Jaimi gave Dane a baleful look. "This is your fault. Before we moved out here, her biggest passion was being able to witness carnage on the school playground."

He grinned, that same devastatingly handsome grin that won her heart a year ago, and every day since. "She loves it."

"I know." Jaimi smiled and leaned back against the seat, thinking about how amazing it had been to see Emily in her first barrel race. She'd been bold and jubilant, exactly like her Grandma. "I love watching her."

Dane smiled. "Me, too." He held out his hand, and she set her hand in his, smiling as he ran his thumb over the platinum wedding band on her left hand, an intimacy that had become a habit she loved. "And I love standing with you, watching her together."

"Me, too." Her heart melted a little bit more, as it did every time she saw Dane's love for Emily shining in his eyes. He hadn't just become her husband. He had become Emily's dad, in every way imaginable. The bond between the two of them was unbreakable, full of laughter, love, and support. It was Dane's coaching that had turned Emily's barrel racing dreams into reality, and he was a wonderful teacher who knew how to keep it fun, while still allowing her to challenge herself.

"It's Ava! There's Ava!" Emily pressed her face up against the window, waving frantically as Dane pulled up in front of Chase's house. He'd barely put the car in park before Emily had unbuckled herself, opened her door, and nearly flung herself out of the truck, shouting for her cousin.

Ava squealed and ran down the steps, meeting Emily halfway. The two seven-year-olds screamed, hugged each other, and then raced up the steps and into Chase's house, disappearing from sight.

Jaimi grinned, her heart feeling so full she couldn't stop smiling. "She loves her cousins so much. It's so beautiful. I didn't grow up with any, and she has so many already."

"Big families are great." Dane leaned over and took her hand. "Merry Christmas, our first as husband and wife."

She smiled. "Merry Christmas to you." He leaned forward and kissed her, a kiss that felt as beautiful and magical as their very first one, on that snowy fence at the festival.

"Hey!" Erin banged on the window, grinning at them. "Save that for home, kiddos. We have a Christmas celebration to help with!"

Jaimi's heart leapt at the sight of Erin. She loved all her sisters-in-law, but she had become especially close to Erin. "Hey!" She opened the door, grinning at the baby in Erin's arms. "Hey, Claire," she crooned. "Are you excited for your first Christmas?"

The little girl just gazed at Jaimi with her big blue eyes, Stockton eyes. She was wearing a green and red knit cap, and her jacket had little jingle bells on it. She grinned at Erin, recognizing the purchases from their most recent shopping trip. "They fit her?"

"A little big, but wearable." Erin glanced over at Dane. "When's Zoey moving back to town? I'm looking forward to meeting her."

"A few weeks." Dane's smile faded, and Jaimi took his hand, knowing how hard the last year had been for his sister, and how hard he'd tried to make it right for her, but he hadn't been able to. He'd wanted a different life for her than the one she'd left behind, but she was coming home, and no one was going to stop her. She'd hung in there for almost a year, since she'd first decided to walk away, but now, she was done, and on her way home.

"Do you need us to pick her up at the airport?" Erin asked.

Dane shook his head. "Ryder has already offered about six times, but she said she's all set. Thanks, though."

Jaimi's heart tightened at how everyone in the Stockton family treated Dane's sister as one of their own. They were such an inclusive family, drawing everyone into their inner circle without hesitation. She felt like she'd been a part of their lives forever, and already, the bond was so tight.

She loved her family, every last one of them. *Thank you, Mom, for giving me the gift of my family.* Somehow, she knew her mom was watching, smiling down from heaven as her solitary, independent daughter found the huge family she'd never realized she wanted or needed.

"How are you feeling?" Erin asked, shifting her baby to her other arm.

"Awesome!" She started to get down from the truck, but before she had begun to move, Dane appeared next to Erin, looking deliciously handsome in his cowboy hat, black jacket and jeans. He never failed to take her breath away. He just looked so incredibly rugged and strong, with kindness etched in every line on his face.

He held his hand out. "Let me help you, sweetheart."

She rolled her eyes. "I'm perfectly capable of getting out of the truck myself."

"I know, but I like to dote on you." He patted her growing belly. "Two kidlets in there isn't good for balance, not when there's snow on the driveway."

"Give the man a break, sis," Steen said cheerfully as he walked up, holding seven shopping bags packed with wrapped presents. "A pregnant wife brings out the protector in us. He won't be able to cope if you don't let him take care of you. Just go with it."

Erin rolled her eyes. "So true. They get worse the further you get along."

"Worse?" Jaimi couldn't keep from smiling. "You mean better?"

Dane grinned. "What? You like it when I go all he-man-protector on you?"

She smiled as she took his hand. "You know I do."

"Yep, I sure do." He slid his arm around her waist as she stepped down, pulling her into his arms for a kiss that made heat spiral through her.

She sighed and beamed at him, loving the feel of his arms around her. "I love you, Dane."

"I know. That makes me the luckiest guy in the world." He grinned, ignoring the shouts of greeting from the house as the other Stocktons noticed their arrival and came out to welcome them. "Because of you, I have everything," he said. "The Stocktons are actually my brothers now, I'm a dad, and, most importantly, I get to spend every day with the woman who fills my heart with love every minute of every day. Forever, my love."

She smiled and draped her arms around his neck. "Forever," she agreed. "That sounds perfect."

~

Did you enjoy Dane and Jaimi's story? If so, please consider leaving a short review on the eTailer and/or Goodreads. Reviews make a huge difference for authors!

~

Do you want to know when Stephanie has a new book out, is running a sale, or giving away prizes? ***Sign up for her private newsletter at www.stephanierowe.com!***

~

ABOUT THE AUTHOR

New York Times and *USA Today* bestselling author Stephanie Rowe is the author of more than forty-five novels, and she's a four-time nominee for the RITA® award, the highest award in romance fiction. As an award-winning author, Stephanie has been touching readers' hearts and keeping them spellbound for more than a decade with her contemporary romances, romantic suspense, paranormal romances, and YA contemporary romances.

For the latest info on Stephanie and her books, connect with her on the web at:

www.stephanierowe.com
stephanie@stephanierowe.com

Made in United States
Orlando, FL
17 April 2022

16928241R00102